MURDER ON HER HONEYMOON

A HANNAH KLINE MYSTERY

PAULA BERNSTEIN

Murder On Her Honeymoon

Third Street Press Publication Date: July 2020

ISBN-13: 978-1-948142-49-6 (E-BOOKS)
ISBN-13: 978-1-948142-50-2 (PRINT BOOKS)

Dedicated to my brother Lawrence Kreisman.

1

Dr. Hannah Kline leaned on the railing as the ferry moved away from the dock, glancing at her new husband, Detective Daniel Ross.

"Nothing makes me happier than the prospect of an entire week without midnight phone calls, births or murders," she said.

Daniel drew her close. "Ready for our honeymoon?"

"More than ready. I can't believe we're married. How did you hear about this place?"

"When I was in the military, I was stationed at Fort Lewis near Tacoma. The San Juan Islands were a favorite spot when I had a weekend off. This island, Oriole, was off the beaten track. Nice beaches. Great hiking trails, and back then, no tourists."

"And now?"

"The major change is that a famous chef opened a B&B and began serving fabulous farm-to-table food. People from Bellingham and Seattle take the ferry over just for dinner. We can spend an entire week doing nothing but reading, sleeping, taking walks along the beach, eating, and making love."

"That sounds like a perfect honeymoon. I hope it doesn't rain."

Daniel grinned. "I think I mentioned several indoor activities in case it rains."

He drew her into the protection of his chest and arms, and they watched as the hills of Oriole Island drew closer. Daniel leaned down and kissed her.

"I'm so happy we're having a baby together. I promise to be the best father ever."

"You already are. Zoe adores you. She still doesn't understand why we aren't taking her on our honeymoon."

All too soon, Hannah heard the ferry loudspeaker giving them a five minute warning. They climbed down the narrow stairs and waited in their car as the ship maneuvered into its berth. Once it had docked, the short line of cars proceeded in an orderly fashion down the ramp and up a dirt road, past a sign that read: *Welcome to Oriole Island, Population 242*, and to the town's main drag.

"Who lives here?" Hannah asked.

"Farmers, artists, retirees, and people who service the vacationers. It's too long a commute to live here and work in Bellingham or Seattle, so it's just locals."

She examined the map on her phone. A two-lane highway circled the island and two roads cut across it. Everything else looked like dirt driveways.

Daniel drove through the main part of town. Once they passed the small commercial center, Hannah could see rustic wood cottages tucked among the tall evergreens and occupied beachfront property on the other side of the road. The dark sand beaches were rocky and dotted with driftwood. Evergreens alternated with groves of alder trees, their leaves an autumn yellow, and white birch trunks stood out among the shadows. There were occasional maples, leaves now a deep red. Where the trees thinned, Hannah caught a glimpse of cultivated fields, gentle hills and occasional cows.

Daniel turned a corner to a beautiful view of sparkling water and the mountains of the Olympic Peninsula. Hannah took a deep breath. She could feel her heart rate slowing, her muscles relaxing, and her blood pressure dropping twenty points. This was what she'd needed; perfect tranquility, even if only for a week.

A few minutes more brought them to a turnoff, where a meandering driveway led up to a white Victorian house on a hill. There was a view in all directions and an expansive front porch furnished with white Adirondack chairs.

"Welcome to Alder House, Sweetheart," Daniel said.

Daniel parked the car close to the front door and they entered the foyer. It had a high ceiling and polished dark wood floors. A young woman sat behind an old-fashioned mahogany desk, her attention on a computer terminal. She raised her head as the door opened.

As they approached, Daniel realized the receptionist was older than his first impression, closer to forty than twenty. She had a thin face and wore no makeup. Her eyes were blue with pale brows and lashes, and fine lines at the corners. Her nose was small and pert, her lips slightly chapped, and when she spoke, he could see a midline space between her front teeth. Her straight blonde hair was cut into a chin-length bob and was beginning to show a few strands of silver. Her only adornment was a dangling pair of bright green feather earrings. Something about her was vaguely familiar.

"Can I help you?" Her eyes scanned him, head to toe.

"I'm Daniel Ross. We have reservations for the week."

"Oh, yes. You have our largest room, the Empire. You mentioned you were on your honeymoon when you made the reservation." She typed in a computer entry and handed him an old-fashioned brass key. Retrieving a second one from the desk drawer, she held it out to Hannah.

"Mrs. Ross?"

Hannah startled, clearly unused to being addressed by that name. Daniel wondered if she'd say something, but she just extended her hand for the key.

"Let me show you around." When the woman stood up, Daniel noticed she was wearing a black turtleneck underneath a shapeless denim jumper that fell to mid-calf and a pair of sturdy boots.

They followed her to the living room, which was anchored by an ornate Victorian fireplace. "We serve wine and appetizers here at five-thirty in the afternoon," she said.

Adjacent to the living room was a dining area furnished with a long table.

"Buffet breakfast is from seven-thirty to nine in the morning, and you'll be having dinner here as well during the week. We eat family style so our guests have a chance to get to know one another. Our restaurant is in an annex at the back of the house. We're open to the public only on weekends now that the summer season is over."

"No ten-course tasting menus during the week?" Daniel asked.

"I'm afraid not, but the food will be prepared by our chef and I promise it will be the same quality as you'll have this coming weekend. Let's go upstairs. I'll have your luggage brought to your room."

They climbed a curved staircase with an ornate wood handrail and were escorted to a door at the end of the second floor hall.

"Here you are." The woman turned to go.

"Thank you," Hannah said. "By the way, I didn't get your name."

"It's Melanie," she said. "Melanie Wells."

Daniel watched her as she walked down the hall. The name had jarred a memory loose. He had a sudden image of a young smiling face, eyes emphasized by blue eye shadow and dark mascara, pink cheeks and cherry lip gloss, hip-length golden hair cascading over naked breasts. He remembered now, lying beneath her as she rode him to climax. He flushed. How could he have failed to recognize her and how could she possibly be here, haunting his honeymoon?

2

HANNAH TURNED THE KEY AND OPENED the door.

"Is it my turn to carry you over the threshold?" she asked, turning to face him.

But Daniel's back was to her. He appeared to be watching Melanie as she walked down the hall. At Hannah's question he turned and smiled.

"Not unless you want a slipped disc."

He draped an arm over her shoulders as they entered.

"It's lovely, Daniel."

"The alternative had burgundy flocked wallpaper. I'm glad you approve of my choice, Mrs. Ross."

Hannah smiled. "I'm happy to be introduced as Mrs. Ross this week. I'm enjoying the anonymity. No one we meet will ask me medical questions or feel obliged to share all the details of her most recent delivery."

Hannah had decided not to change her name when she married Daniel. She'd done it once before, after her wedding to Ben. It hadn't occurred to her then that she had a choice, and she hadn't anticipated all the paperwork involved. This time was different. She'd been Dr. Hannah Kline to all her patients and colleagues for far too long to assume another identity.

Hannah shut the door behind them. The room was huge. In its center was a four-poster bed with a canopy. The bedding had a blue and white floral pattern, which echoed the colors of the Oriental rug. Two indigo velvet armchairs with ottomans and standing reading lamps flanked a fireplace with a white marble mantel. At the other end, a semi-circular sitting area in front of large windows let in the light. The walls were painted pale blue with white trim. An antique desk and chair sat in the corner. The room projected tranquility and romance, devoid of Victorian clutter. She loved it.

Daniel was staring out the window at the view of the water. He seemed distracted. Hannah wondered if it had anything to do with the sour-faced receptionist. She watched him for a while and then retreated to the bathroom. As she emerged there was a knock at the door. Daniel opened it to reveal a tall, gangly, teenaged boy with their suitcases. She wondered if he was Melanie's son. He had the same blue eyes and pert nose but a head of unruly dark hair.

"Where do you want these?" he asked.

"Just leave them," Daniel said, reaching for his wallet.

He handed the boy a five-dollar bill and closed the door after him. Daniel lifted the bags and put them on the bed.

"Shall we unpack?" he asked.

"Sure." She was feeling a little disconcerted. She'd been expecting Daniel to put her on the bed, not the suitcases.

They busied themselves hanging and folding, and putting toiletries in the bathroom. When they finished, she glanced at her watch. It was already 4:30.

"I think I'll take a quick shower and change before we go downstairs. We didn't get any lunch and I'm hungry," she said.

"Sounds good. While you're doing that, I'll stretch my legs and take a short walk. I'm stiff from all that sitting in the plane."

He deposited a kiss on her forehead and left.

3

DANIEL WALKED DOWN THE STAIRS TO the foyer. Melanie was there, seated at her desk. She looked up at him.

"Is everything satisfactory?"

"Everything's fine. I just realized that we've met before. You probably don't remember me. It was years ago in Tacoma, when I was at Fort Lewis. You were working as a waitress at this bar not far from the base."

"I remember you. I recognized your name when you made the reservation." She looked up at him, unsmiling. It was a bit unnerving.

"Then I apologize for not recognizing you right away. You cut your hair."

She shrugged. "It was too much work, taking care of all that hair. I didn't expect you to remember me. It was just a one night stand."

It had been a one-night stand, the most exciting sex he'd had in a long time, and the next day he'd been wracked with guilt about being unfaithful to his wife, Annie. He hadn't returned to the bar, afraid he'd be tempted again, and he'd been decommissioned shortly afterwards. He'd thought about her occasionally, when he needed a good erotic fantasy, and wondered what had happened to her. Now he knew. He was relieved that she no longer possessed that incredible sex appeal.

"Yes, well it's nice to see you again. Do you own this place?"

"Half of it. The house and the adjacent farm belonged to my grandparents. I inherited it. Scott Nilsson, our chef, bought a half interest from me. He provided the money to renovate the place and the cachet to make our restaurant a huge success. We're partners."

"That's terrific," Daniel said. "I can't wait to try his food. I'm glad you've done so well."

She didn't respond, didn't ask him anything about himself. An awkward silence ensued.

"Well, I'm going to take a walk. See you later," Daniel said, as he slipped out the front door.

He could have sworn he felt Melanie staring after him.

Melanie watched as Daniel walked down the hill and crossed the highway to the beach. She hadn't been certain, when she saw his name on the registration list, if it belonged to the same young lieutenant she'd found so attractive. He hadn't changed much, was still fit and well-built with thick dark hair and piercing blue eyes. The only sign of age was some gray on his sideburns and at his temples, and a few wrinkles around his eyes when he smiled. She hadn't expected to feel so angry and agitated when she saw him again. It had only been a one-time screw, but that one time had been memorable. The sexual chemistry had been so intense they'd practically ripped one another's clothes off and fell into bed. A few weeks later, when he failed to return to the bar, she discovered he'd been discharged and had resumed his civilian life. Now he was married to that redhead.

She reached for her purse, in the file drawer of her desk, and examined her face in a small mirror. No wonder Daniel hadn't recognized her. Hard work and motherhood had aged her. She made an effort to look attractive at first, when Scott arrived on the scene, but stopped trying when it became apparent that his real interest was in the restaurant and not in her. Glancing at her watch, she realized it was time to get the hors d'oeuvres and wine organized for the guests. Locking the file drawer, she got up and headed for the kitchen.

Daniel walked along the beach, picking up and discarding smooth pebbles, shells, and pieces of driftwood. Seeing Melanie again had rattled him and he wasn't sure why. Surely all that was ancient history and shouldn't even be allowed to enter his mind on his honeymoon with Hannah. Glancing at his watch, he headed back, and was relieved to see that no one was at the front desk when he returned to the inn.

Hannah had changed to a pair of black slacks and a dark green cashmere sweater. Her long red hair had been brushed smooth and she was applying blush and lipstick when he entered the room.

"Hi, sweetie. Have a nice walk?"

"I did. I'm going to put on something clean and wolf down some appetizers with you."

Hannah sat in one of the armchairs and watched as he put on a crisp blue shirt.

"You've been looking very serious," she said. "Is something wrong?"

"Not really. That receptionist looked familiar and I was wracking my brain trying to remember where I'd seen her before."

"Not on a wanted poster, I hope?"

"Nothing that dramatic. It finally came to me. I'd known her when I was in the army. She was a waitress at a bar that was popular with the officers."

"I hope she was nicer to people when she was a waitress. She barely cracked a smile when she was checking us in."

"I guess she doesn't get tips for checking people in. Are you ready to go?" He held out his hand and helped her out of the deep armchair.

"I'm starved," she said. "What do you think the chef is making for dinner?"

4

Chef Scott Nilsson surveyed his kingdom with satisfaction. The first thing he had done after investing in this house was to gut the old farmhouse kitchen and replace it with stainless steel, professional grade appliances. Luke Murray, his sous-chef, was busy chopping garden vegetables and preparing the appetizers for this evening. He'd chosen little puff pastries with locally made blue cheese and fig jam, skewers of teriyaki salmon, locally caught, and mini tostada shells filled with ceviche. Scott himself was preparing tonight's dinner. He needed to impress his special guest who would, he hoped, take his ambitions to the next level.

"What are the wines for tonight?" Melanie rushed through the kitchen door and opened the wine refrigerator.

"I've taken them out already," Scott said, elbowing her aside. "We're having the Chateau St. Michelle 2015 Eroica Riesling and the 2011 Cave B Cabernet Franc."

"Isn't that a waste of expensive wine for a Monday night?" she argued.

"Not tonight. We have a guest I want to impress."

"Who?"

"Later," he said. "Luke's got the appetizers ready to set out."

He handed her two bottles of Riesling and the ice bucket. Grabbing the Cabernet, he followed her out of the kitchen to the living room, where they placed the wine behind the mini bar and set out the red and white wine glasses. Luke followed them, arranging trays and little plates on the library table.

"Why don't you change into something nicer and put on a little makeup? You look worn out," Scott said.

"Maybe I am worn out." She glared at him. Without another word, she stormed out in the direction of the administrative office, where she kept extra clothes and toilet articles.

Scott was finding her more and more annoying. He had fallen in love with the house and the farm the moment he'd seen them. If only Melanie hadn't come with them. She'd refused to sell him the whole property, and his only way in had been to seduce her, literally and figuratively, into a partnership. She'd been adept in bed, but he was getting increasingly tired of the duty fucks. If things worked out tonight, he wouldn't need her anymore. Tonight's dinner should seal the deal with his prospective new partner, Craig Sutton.

Craig Sutton looked in the mirror and was satisfied. His craggy, suntanned face was still handsome at fifty-five and his body was in excellent shape for his age. His black cashmere turtleneck sweater and gray merino wool Giorgio Armani pants gave exactly the impression of casual wealth that he wanted to portray. He ran a comb through his beautifully cut, thick gray hair and turned to examine his wife, Angela.

She was sitting in front of the fireplace, reading a travel magazine, wearing winter white designer slacks and a matching silk blouse. Her dark hair was cut short, in a pixie style, and her face, thanks to regular Botox treatments, was free of wrinkles. She wore chunky gold earrings and a matching bracelet. Sensing his stare, she looked up and smiled.

"Don't you look like the cover of GQ?"

"Glad you approve. Ready for some wine and food?"

"Absolutely. Is there anything else to do on this island besides eat?"

Angela was a city girl. Several days of bucolic rest was not her idea of a fun vacation and he hadn't yet told her why they were here.

"I'm afraid not, but I'm here for business, not pleasure."

"What kind of business?"

"This obscure restaurant in the middle of nowhere has been remarkably successful. Think of how much money could be made by opening a few more, under the chef's name and supervision, in more urban locations. We could have a Nilsson's in Seattle, in Portland, maybe in San Francisco."

"So you're going to propose that you finance them, he runs them, and you share the profits, in your favor, of course."

Craig smiled. "Precisely. What do you think?"

"Brilliant, if you can coax him off his island."

"Somehow, I don't think that will be very difficult, providing his food lives up to its reputation."

5

Samantha Allen fortified herself with two fingers of scotch from her personal stash. She was going to need it tonight. Who would have imagined that Scott Nilsson would end up on an obscure island, owning a successful restaurant? She'd thought that by now he'd be in jail.

When her friend and fellow writer Kylie Evans had suggested Alder house for their annual writer's retreat, Samantha had looked it up online and was shocked to find the name of her nemesis. She had never met Nilsson in person, and he wouldn't recognize her name.

Samantha maintained a low profile without photos on the web. She didn't need Facebook or Twitter to sell her wildly popular historical romance novels, and her short, stocky, overweight body and close cropped gray hair didn't match her nom-de-plume. Why disillusion her millions of readers who no doubt imagined her as a tall willowy blonde?

What was more important, she didn't want any of her academic colleagues in the History Department at the University of Chicago to know that Professor Mildred Hunter wrote steamy sex scenes on the side. Samantha finished off her scotch, wrapped herself in a royal blue wool poncho that covered all her figure flaws, put her brass key in the pocket of her pants and headed downstairs to meet her fellow guests.

Literary novelist Kylie Evans had no intention of numbing her palate with alcohol. She was here on a mission that included, but was not restricted to finishing off her latest novel. Kylie had been a tall, curvy brunette in her twenties. At fifty, she was somewhat less curvy and had switched to ash blonde to hide the gray.

The combination of wealth, health, an excellent dermatologist and a first-rate hair dresser kept her looking youthful and glamorous. For the evening, she wore designer jeans, a form-fitting black leotard, and a casual black leather jacket.

Her husband, George, owner of a large, high end restaurant franchise, had thought it a brilliant idea to combine Kylie's writing retreat with an anonymous opportunity to sample the food at Alder House. Kylie's culinary training had come in handy as they built their restaurant empire, and would continue to do so. Neither one of them had any scruples about replicating the finest dishes of other chefs. Kylie doubted that Scott Nilsson would recognize her, but she remembered him, and not too fondly. A final glance in the mirror, and one more coating of lipstick and she was ready.

Ilana Flores sat in her room, clenching and unclenching her hands. Why had she allowed her three fellow writers to talk her into coming here?

"It's the perfect place to inspire you," Kylie had said. "It could be the next setting for one of your clever culinary mysteries."

It was hard to argue with that, and the other three had been enthusiastic. Ilana had worked under Scott Nilsson when he was the chef at a prominent Seattle restaurant, years ago, and she hated him. What if he remembered her, and humiliated her yet again in front of her friends? Then again, why should he remember her? She was just another Latina kitchen slave taking shouted orders in his kitchen, just another anonymous figure in a white apron and hair covering.

Ilana was wearing her curly hair, with its strands of gray, loose. Her olive skin and dark eyes were untouched by makeup and she wore a long gray skirt with a flowing tie-dye shirt. It was a hippie look and she felt comfortable in the loose, concealing clothes. Of course he wouldn't remember her, and she'd get her revenge by modeling her next murder victim after him.

Vanessa Brooks still couldn't believe how lucky she was to be the youngest and newest member of this prestigious writing retreat group. She'd met the others at a writer's conference two years ago. Samantha lived in Chicago. Kylie and Ilana worked in Portland, and she herself was the manager of a boutique hotel in Seattle.

The other three were published and recognized. Vanessa was writing a memoir and struggling with writer's block. At the conference, the four had been together in a workshop where each of them read excerpts from their current projects. Samantha had approached her later in the day and invited her to share a drink with them.

"We were all so impressed with your writing," Samantha had said. "Memoir is the most difficult genre. It's so deeply personal, and so hard to expose yourself and your deepest fears and feelings to an audience of readers who might not appreciate your work."

Vanessa had relaxed and smiled. She'd been completely

entranced by this warm, caring older woman. "I appreciate the encouragement. This is the first time I've read any of my work to anyone."

"The three of us have been talking about you," Kylie said. "We all think you are exceptionally talented, and we'd like to ask if you'd care to join us on our annual writer's retreat."

"We get together for a week every year," Ilana added, "to work on our current books in a tranquil setting and to give one another constructive feedback. It's always energizing."

Vanessa had felt incredibly flattered that three successful, published writers were willing to take her under their wing. She'd accepted without hesitation. Last year's retreat had been amazing and she'd made significant progress on her book.

Alder House had seemed a wonderful choice for this year and she'd readily agreed. It wasn't until she checked online, and saw the name Scott Nilsson, that she realized this week could be a disaster.

The chapters she'd been unable to tackle, because they were so painful, were all about Scott. She dreaded going downstairs and coming face to face with him. Of course, he'd never recognize her. Perhaps this was a good thing. Actually seeing him could be the breakthrough her memoir needed.

Vanessa checked her reflection. She looked as she always did: young, professional, calm. Her light brown hair swirled around her shoulders. Her arresting blue eyes were emphasized with a touch of blue shadow and black mascara. She wore her good black wool pants and a pink sweater set. She completed the look by putting on a pair of fake pearl stud earrings. Taking a deep breath, she grabbed her key and her purse and left the room.

Noel Gunderson finished shaving, both his face and his head, buttoned his green plaid flannel shirt, and pulled the leather belt with its silver buckle a little tighter to secure his jeans. Sitting down, he fastened his Doc Martens and grabbed his room key. He could definitely do with a few glasses of wine and some appetizers, and he was looking forward to seeing Melanie.

Noel was a regular at Alder House. He liked to stay for a few days, three or four times a year, preferring off season when the island was less crowded with day tourists and there was less competition for the fishing boats.

Noel was passionate about fishing and a skilled hunter. There wasn't much to hunt on the island, so he pursued that hobby elsewhere. On Oriole Island, the only game he stalked was Melanie Wells. Melanie enjoyed being hunted, and even more, she liked being caught. Noel had his share of sexual partners but none of them was as hot and as imaginative as Melanie. He could hardly wait to fuck her again. It was going to be a great week.

6

As Hannah and Daniel descended the stairs they could hear the murmur of voices in the main lounge.

"Let's go incognito," Hannah whispered. Whenever she told people what she did for a living, she was bombarded with other people's health issues.

Daniel gave her a puzzled look.

"If anyone wants to know what we do, I'm a bookkeeper and you do data analysis. That way no one will ask about your latest murder case or want my medical advice."

He laughed. "What do I do if one of those people actually knows something about databases?"

"You change the subject to their profession. People always prefer talking about themselves to listening to you. We're just a honeymoon couple."

"Okay, undercover it is."

They walked, hand in hand, into the main lounge. Hannah noticed a group of middle-aged women near the bar where Melanie was pouring wine. Melanie had put on some makeup and a black jersey dress. It was a considerable improvement.

A handsome gray-haired man in a black sweater was helping himself at the generously stocked appetizer table, and chatting with a fellow in a plaid flannel shirt. Sitting apart was an elegant woman in winter white clothes and too much jewelry, who was sipping a glass of white wine and looking bored.

"Drink?" Daniel asked.

Hannah nodded, and they made their way to the wine.

"One white, one red," Daniel said to Melanie. Her face was expressionless as she handed him two glasses.

"Delicious," Hannah said as she sipped her ice cold Riesling. She'd have to switch to Perrier after this. She wasn't allowing herself more than one glass of wine per week while she was pregnant.

"We try to choose wines worthy of our food," Melanie said.

"You must be the honeymoon couple." A short, plump, gray-haired woman smiled at them. "I'm Samantha Allen."

"I'm Hannah. This is my husband Daniel Ross. How did you know?" Hannah asked.

"There are only two couples here and you were the ones holding hands."

"Excellent detective work," Daniel said.

"How did you meet?" Samantha asked. "I'm always interested in origin stories. I write Romance novels."

"I'm afraid our story isn't very romantic. Match.com," Hannah said. She wasn't about to tell this perfect stranger that Daniel had been the lead homicide detective assigned to the murder of her sister-in-law.

Samantha sighed. "The internet has certainly reduced the number of 'meet cutes'. Come meet my friends. We're here on a writer's retreat."

She gestured at three women sitting on a sofa, their plates piled high. Daniel and Hannah helped themselves to food and followed Samantha to the opposite sofa.

"Hey, everyone, meet Daniel and Hannah. They're on their honeymoon. This is Ilana, Kylie and Vanessa. Ilana writes fabulous culinary mystery novels. Kylie just published a well-received literary novel, and Vanessa is working on a memoir."

"I'm impressed," Hannah said. "I'm a voracious reader. I always wished I had the talent and the imagination to write."

"It's not so much an issue of talent and imagination," Samantha said. "Writing is about discipline, and the willingness to revise and revise until you can't stand looking at your manuscript anymore."

"Then, just as you think you're done, you hand it to your editor, and discover you have to rewrite it again," Kylie said.

"How do you know when you're done?" Hannah asked.

"You're done when your editor tells you it's good enough. If you insist on perfect, it's never done."

"You still need to have a good idea for a plot and characters. I would think that's the hardest part," Hannah said.

"Not as hard as you might imagine," Ilana said. "There's a cliché, 'write what you know,' and there's a good deal of truth to it. We draw from our experiences and from the people we meet. I work in a restaurant and know a great deal about food. That's why I write culinary mysteries."

"And I have affairs with dark, handsome, brooding, mysterious men who sweep me off my feet," Samantha added.

Everyone laughed.

"Laugh, you may," Samantha agreed, "but my settings are authentic. I love to go to exotic places and research their histories, so that my romances are about more than just sex, although I do include plenty of that. I must know a hundred synonyms for *hot throbbing member*."

Hannah glanced at her husband. Was that a flush she saw on his face? Clearly, he wasn't used to girl talk.

Just then a bell rang and Melanie announced that dinner was being served in the dining room.

There were nine elegant place settings at the long table and the guests distributed themselves. The four writers faced one another at one end. Hannah seated herself between Daniel and Kylie, and opposite the other couple. She hoped there would be some interesting conversation. Mr. Flannel-Shirt chose the head of the table and leaned back as if he were the host.

Daniel turned toward him and offered a handshake. "I'm Daniel Ross. This is my wife Hannah."

"Noel Gunderson."

"Craig Sutton," said the handsome gray-haired man. "My wife, Angela."

Hannah smiled at Angela. "Pleased to meet you."

At that moment, a man wearing a pristine white apron and tall chef's hat entered the room. The crowd quieted.

"Welcome, everyone. I'm Scott Nilsson, your host and chef. We've planned a special fall dinner for you tonight and I hope you enjoy it. Our lovely waitress Grace will be serving you. To begin with, an amuse-bouche, curried squash soup."

An attractive young blonde in a black waitress uniform entered the room carrying a tray, which she placed on the sideboard. Circling the table, she distributed espresso cups containing a thick orange soup, garnished with crème frâiche and chives. As she leaned over to place one in front of Gunderson, he squeezed her rear end.

"Thanks, Sweetheart."

The girl winced and grabbing his wrist, replaced his hand on the table.

Daniel shot him a look. "It's bad manners to manhandle the staff."

"Who are you, the police?" Gunderson said. "Gracie doesn't mind. She knows me. I'm a regular."

"Well, I mind," Hannah said. "Being felt up by the guests isn't in the job description for a waitress."

If there was anything she detested, it was an entitled male sexual predator.

"You go, girl," Samantha said. The rest of the writing group toasted Hannah with their espresso cups.

Grace flushed, gave Hannah a tiny smile, and retreated with her tray to the kitchen.

"Looks like you're outnumbered," Daniel said.

Gunderson glowered and reached for the bread basket.

Grace reentered the dining room with an empty tray and began clearing the espresso cups. She gave Gunderson a wide berth as she took his plate. Then she brought in a tray of salads, which she served first to the six women. The salads were a composition of pink grapefruit, avocado, dates, goat cheese and pistachios in a fruity vinaigrette dressing. Everyone dug in.

The tension decreased and finally Craig Sutton broke the silence.

"So, where are you from?" he asked Daniel.

"Los Angeles. Yourself?"

"Seattle. I'm a venture capitalist. I find successful start-up businesses and help them expand."

"You must be very popular."

"He is," Angela said.

"Are you involved in the business?" Hannah asked.

"Not really. I just help Craig entertain his clients and network. Do you work with your husband?"

That was an interesting question, but to answer it truthfully, she'd have to reveal the fact that Daniel was a homicide detective and she'd helped him solve quite a few cases.

"Daniel's a data analyst," Hannah said. "I do bookkeeping. There isn't much overlap."

"What about you, Gunderson?" Craig Sutton asked. "You from around here? You mentioned you come often to Alder House."

Gunderson turned toward him, ignoring Daniel. "I'm a sportsman. I come here three or four times a year to hunt and fish. Scott will cook anything I bring back. The guy's a genius with salmon and venison."

"You have your own boat?" Sutton asked.

"I rent when I'm here. You?"

"We have a little yacht, The Angela, but I didn't bring her this weekend."

Hannah caught Daniel's eye and raised her eyebrows. Perhaps at breakfast they could sit at the other end with the writing group.

The next course was a lavender sorbet, just to cleanse everyone's palate. When she finished, Hannah excused herself and headed for the Ladies Room.

Grace was just exiting as Hannah arrived.

"I hope I didn't embarrass you. I'm Hannah, by the way."

"My name's Grace." She gave Hannah a tentative smile. "Thanks for speaking up. I've tried complaining to Miss Wells but she never does anything. I think she doesn't want to lose a regular customer."

"You shouldn't have to put up with that kind of behavior."

"I doubt he'll try again, at least not on this visit. I'll make sure you get an extra-large dessert."

Just what she needed. Other women got nauseous during pregnancy and kept their weight gain under control. She, on the other hand, felt like eating anything that wasn't tied down. Thinking about dessert had Hannah wondering what the main course was.

When she returned to her seat, she found a plate of short ribs with mashed potatoes and roasted brussel sprouts awaiting her. Everyone was digging in, except for Angela, who was eating salmon. There was always someone in every crowd who didn't eat red meat, or poultry, or was a vegan or gluten-free. It must be complicated running a restaurant and having to please everyone. She took a large bite of the rib. It was divine.

"Leave room for dessert," Daniel whispered.

"Our baby will always have room for dessert," Hannah said.

As the guests gobbled up the short ribs, Luke Murray, the sous-chef, put the finishing touches on the miniature blueberry crisps in the kitchen. They would be served with homemade vanilla bean ice cream. Scott Nilsson had retreated to a comfortable chair in the corner, from which he could watch his minions finish the serving and cleanup while he sipped a glass of his favorite cognac.

This was going to be Luke's last year at Alder House. He'd paid his dues and he was tired of being under Nilsson's thumb. The guy might be a genius as a chef, but he was a bastard as a human being. The only nice part of the job was Luke's girlfriend, Grace.

Grace had just come in from serving the ribs and was standing at the sink, rinsing the salad plates and loading them into the dishwasher. Her lips were tightly compressed and she was shoving the plates into their slots as if she wanted to break them.

"Anything wrong?" he whispered, coming up behind her.

"Gunderson," she said. "That prick doesn't know how to keep his hands to himself."

"What did he do?" Luke asked.

"Squeezed my ass."

"Would you like me to hit him in the balls with a frying pan? It would be my pleasure."

Grace laughed. "That honeymoon couple told him off and the other women practically applauded. He's in a pretty crappy mood. It's about time."

"I think it's about time for both of us to get out of here. I've started looking for a new job and as soon as I find one, I'm splitting. Why don't you quit and come with me?"

Grace gave him a big smile. "That's the best offer I've had all day, but first I have to serve the dessert."

After dessert, Scott Nilsson, seated in a kitchen nook and sipping from his glass of cognac, awaited the arrival of Craig Sutton. As Craig entered the room, Scott waved him over.

"I wanted to compliment you on the meal. It was superb," Craig said, with a handshake.

"Glad you enjoyed it. Would you care to top it off with a drink?"

As Nilsson was pouring, he noticed Craig glancing at an open box of artisan truffles on the counter. It seemed that everyone had a weakness for good chocolate.

"Have one," Scott said. "The staff has been nibbling them all evening."

Indeed, half the box was already empty. Craig helped himself.

"A perfect end to a perfect meal," he said. "Can we have a private word?"

"Of course. Come into my office."

Nilsson's office was a small room just off the kitchen with a desk and shelves lined with cookbooks. He motioned Sutton to a chair.

"Have you given some thought to my proposal?" Sutton asked. "Nilsson's Seattle would be a sensation, and we could have it open by the end of the year. I've found the perfect space near the Pike Street market, a restaurant that went out of business. The kitchen is new. All it needs is some interior design."

"I have thought about it. If our lawyers can finalize a contract, I'm in. Melanie can run this place. The recipes are tested. All we'd have to do is hire a substitute chef. I can come supervise once a month or so to make sure the quality hasn't deteriorated."

"What about your sous-chef? Could he take over?"

Nilsson sipped some more cognac and rolled his eyes. "I doubt it. It would be an example of the Peter Principle, allowing an employee to rise to his level of incompetence. Luke's a good subordinate but he hasn't any imagination."

"Well, I'm sure you won't have trouble hiring someone. Let's talk further tomorrow morning, so we're both clear on the deal we want, and then we can call our lawyers."

Nilsson rose and shook hands. "I look forward to it."

As Sutton left the kitchen, Nilsson was smiling. All he had to do now was figure out how to break the news to Melanie.

After dinner, Noel Gunderson slipped out the side door and walked along the dirt road toward the farmhouse. Melanie was expecting him, and it was late enough so that her son would be in his room, listening to loud music with his headphones on. They wouldn't be disturbed.

The front door was unlocked and he went in, heading toward her bedroom. He didn't bother to knock. Melanie was in bed, watching some dumb comedy. She was wearing a low cut, black silk nightgown, the one he especially liked because he could see most of her tits. He'd have her out of it in a minute.

She smiled when she saw him and got out of bed, offering a prolonged tongue kiss. "Have a nice dinner?"

"Food was fine. Company sucked. That redhead has a big mouth, her husband is obnoxious, and those women are a bunch of dikes."

He didn't really think that was true. Maybe just the old, fat, gray-haired one. He wouldn't have minded getting it on with one or two of the others.

"Poor baby. Come here where you are appreciated."

He slid his hands under her nightgown and squeezed her bare buttocks.

"Would you object if I squeezed your ass?"

"Do you hear me complaining?"

"I guess not." Gunderson picked her up and carried her back to the bed. He'd feel better after a good fuck. It was just what he needed to get himself ready for a long day of fishing.

7

Daniel awoke to the sound of a scream. At first, he thought he was dreaming but the scream came again. He jumped out of bed, slid his feet into his sneakers and ran for the door in his pajamas. Hannah, in her nightgown, robe and slippers was not far behind.

The scream had subsided into loud sobs coming from the direction of the kitchen. Daniel motioned Hannah to stay back and opened the door.

Grace was standing in the middle of the kitchen, staring at a figure in the corner chair. Daniel came up behind her.

"Grace, what is it?"

She turned toward him, face streaked with tears.

"Our chef. I think he's dead."

Scott Nilsson was slumped sideways, his arms hanging over the sides of the chair. His face was blue and Daniel could see that the lower parts of both arms were deep blue as well, suggesting that he had died in that position and the blood had had enough time to pool. A small side table had fallen to the floor, spilling broken glass, alcohol, and a scatter of chocolates on the ground. The smell of feces and decomposition was obvious.

"Did you touch him?" he asked.

Grace shook her head.

"Come with me. We shouldn't be in here. We need to notify the police."

Daniel put his arm around her shoulders and guided her into the dining room. He turned to Hannah.

"Scott Nilsson is dead. Grace, is there a police station on the island? I've never noticed one."

"There isn't one. You have to call Bellingham. Nothing ever happens here."

"Are you suspecting a homicide?" Hannah asked.

"I didn't get close enough to the body to make any judgment about how he died. But it needs to be treated as a suspicious death until a medical examiner has had a chance to evaluate him."

Hannah turned to Grace. "It must have been awful for you, walking into the kitchen and finding him. Did he have any medical problems that you know of?"

"He wasn't the sort to confide in the help. You might ask Miss Wells. She knows him the best."

"Can you remember the last time you saw him alive?" Daniel asked.

"It was about ten o'clock. Luke and I finished cleaning up the dinner dishes and set the table for breakfast. Scott was talking to one of the guests in his office, the good-looking man with the gray hair. After he left, Scott sat down in that chair with a bottle of cognac and the rest of the box of chocolates. He always ends his evenings with cognac. That's when Luke and I headed home."

"Do you both live locally?" Hannah asked.

"I live with my parents. They own the café in town. Luke has a tiny cottage near the beach."

Daniel looked at his watch. It was barely 5:30 a.m. "You get here early."

"Breakfast starts at seven. I was just about to put up the coffee."

Hannah sighed. "I guess there won't be any breakfast for anyone this morning."

"What the hell is going on here?" Noel Gunderson stalked into the dining room with Craig Sutton not far behind him. Daniel could hear voices descending the stairs. Clearly, everyone was awake.

"We've had a death," Hannah said. "Mr. Nilsson, in the kitchen."

"Oh, no," Sutton said.

Gunderson started to walk toward the door. Daniel blocked him.

"No one should go in there. The police need to be notified and the kitchen has to be treated as a potential crime scene until the medical examiner arrives."

By this time, all the other guests had come downstairs and were listening.

"Who made you the boss?" Gunderson said.

"I'm a homicide detective with the Los Angeles Police Department," Daniel said. "And the quickest way to piss off the Bellingham police is if all of you leave trace evidence in the kitchen."

Gunderson backed off.

Just then, the front door opened and a young man in jeans and a T-shirt, with bright red hair, entered the dining room.

"Grace, what's going on here?" he asked.

Grace looked at Daniel. "This is Luke Murray, our sous-chef."

Daniel held out his hand. "Daniel Ross."

"Mr. Ross is one of our guests and a homicide detective from Los Angeles. I found Scott this morning, dead in the kitchen. Mr. Ross said none of us should go in there."

"Was he murdered?" Luke asked, his eyes wide.

"Probably a natural death, but until we know for sure, it's

best not to touch anything." Daniel turned to Hannah. "Could you go and phone the Bellingham police? I left my cell in our room. I'll wait here."

"Of course."

"Is Melanie here yet? Does she know?" Luke asked.

"She hasn't come in," Grace said. "Maybe you should call her."

"Me?" Luke looked horrified at the thought.

"I can call her if you'd prefer," Daniel offered.

"Please," Luke said. He handed Daniel his cell phone with Melanie's contact information.

Daniel turned toward the crowd in the dining room. "May I suggest that for now you all return to your rooms? There isn't anything you can do here that will be helpful until the police arrive."

"I hate to be self-centered in the face of a tragedy," Samantha said, "but if the kitchen is off limits, does that mean no food today for any of us?" She was wearing a ratty flannel bathrobe and her gray hair stuck up in all directions.

"I can call my parents," Grace said. "They own the café. I'm sure they'd be willing to provide coffee and enough baked goods to feed everyone."

"That sounds like a good idea," Daniel said. "Thank you, Grace."

He waited for the guests to go upstairs, took a deep breath, and called Melanie.

"Miss Wells. This is Daniel Ross at the hotel. There's a major problem. Could you please come to Alder House right away?"

"What problem?" She sounded sleepy and annoyed.

"I'd rather tell you in person. It's about Mr. Nilsson."

"I'll be there as soon as I've dressed," she said and hung up.

"You didn't tell her," Luke said.

"This is the kind of news I always try to deliver in person," Daniel said.

"I've called the police," Hannah announced, returning to the dining room. She had put on jeans and a sweater and was carrying two cell phones, one of which she handed to Daniel.

"Detective Elias Lindstrom said he'd be here within the hour. He'll be bringing people to collect the body and any evidence that seems appropriate. He said not to touch anything in the kitchen."

"What about the medical examiner?"

"He'll be notified."

Daniel turned to Luke.

"Do you have any duct tape that we could use to block off the kitchen door?"

"I'll go look," Luke said. He put an arm around Grace. "Why don't you come with me?"

"Can you stay here for five minutes while I go up and change?" Daniel asked Hannah. She would know she was expected to guard the door without him having to spell it out. "Miss Wells is on her way. I should be back before she arrives."

As Daniel ran up the stairs, he wondered why it was that dead bodies seemed to follow them everywhere.

Melanie Wells was not in a good mood. She'd fallen asleep late after some exciting sex and hated being awakened by the phone. Noel had returned to the B&B before morning. Melanie made it a rule that he had to leave well before Josh woke up.

Her son was already dressed and eating cereal in the kitchen.

"Hi, Mom. Who called?"

"They need me at work. Come on. I'll take you to school." Whatever the hell Daniel Ross wanted from her, it could wait.

Josh put his bowl in the sink and grabbed his backpack, while Melanie found her car keys.

When Melanie reached Alder House, she found Daniel and his red-headed wife seated in the dining room. There were two pieces of blue duct tape blocking the door to the kitchen.

"What was so important you had to wake me up?" she demanded.

Daniel stood. "Please, Miss Wells, sit down. I have some bad news."

Melanie sat. As she did, she noticed there was no breakfast on the sideboard and no other guests visible. Something was very wrong.

"When Grace came in this morning to start breakfast, she found Mr. Nilsson in the kitchen chair, dead."

Melanie's jaw dropped. "No, he can't be."

"I'm afraid he is. He appears to have died in the middle of the night. Did he have any medical conditions?"

This was a disaster. How was she ever going to find a chef of his caliber to take over? Everything she'd worked so hard to build would disintegrate.

"Scott was a health freak. He ran five miles every morning. Why are you asking? Did he die of a heart attack? Where is he?"

"We don't know why he died. We called the police in Bellingham. They're sending an officer and a medical examiner. Mr. Nilsson's body is in the kitchen. I put tape across the door so it wouldn't be disturbed."

"Who told you that you could take charge? Where are the rest of my employees? Where's Luke?"

"I'm a homicide detective, Miss Wells, in Los Angeles. I was the first one downstairs when Grace screamed, and I know enough to keep people from touching anything before the police arrive. Luke and Grace went to the café to bring back breakfast for the guests. All we can do now, I'm afraid, is wait for the Bellingham police."

"I'll be in my office," Melanie said. "I need to be alone."

Without a second look at either of them, she got up and walked out.

Detective Elias Lindstrom glanced at his watch and pressed harder on the accelerator of his car. He didn't want to miss the next ferry and have to wait half an hour on the dock.

Next to him, Detective Rashida James, his partner, raised her eyebrows. "He probably just died of a heart attack from eating all that rich food. I don't know why we're even doing this. It could have been assigned to some low-level cop."

"The Chief insisted. Nilsson's the biggest celebrity chef in Washington and he's only 47 years old. If the death is suspicious and we didn't take it seriously, the department will be blasted by the media."

"I hate celebrities," Rashida said. "It's bad enough they get special treatment when they're alive. They can't even die quietly like the rest of us."

"Well said." Elias always liked working with Rashida. She was the only black woman in the department, and she was smart, tough, and never failed to speak her mind.

He looked in his rear view mirror to be sure the coroner's van was still behind him. This was one case that would definitely require an autopsy, regardless of what the medical examiner thought.

8

Elias Lindstrom, Rashida James, and the coroner's van arrived at Alder House at 8:30 a.m. Elias pushed the front door open and found himself in a two-story foyer, facing a middle-aged blonde seated at an antique desk. Her eyes were bloodshot and it was obvious she had been crying.

"I'm Detective Lindstrom," he said, holding out his badge and ID for her inspection. "You are?"

"Melanie Wells. I own Alder House. Scott Nilsson was my chef and partner."

"I'm sorry for your loss, Miss Wells. What can you tell me about Mr. Nilsson's death? When did you last see him alive?"

"About seven o'clock last night. I stopped into the kitchen, said goodnight to everyone and walked home."

"What was Mr. Nilsson doing when you said goodnight?"

"The usual, supervising the staff."

"Are you aware of any medical problems he may have had?"

"No. You could ask his doctor. He gets a checkup once a year in Bellingham."

Lindstrom reached into his pocket and retrieved a small notebook. "Do you have his doctor's name?"

"I don't, but I imagine you can find it in his cell phone."

"How did you learn he had died?"

"One of the guests called, woke me, and told me when I got here. I was, am shocked."

"Which guest was that?"

"Daniel Ross. He's a homicide detective from Los Angeles. He made sure no one went into the kitchen until you got here."

"Where is he now?"

"Dining room."

"Thank you, Miss Wells. We'll speak later." Elias hoped the homicide detective would be more helpful than Melanie Wells.

When Elias walked into the main lounge, followed by Rashida, he found it occupied by a group of silent guests, drinking coffee and helping themselves to pastries on the sideboard.

"Are you the police?" The question came from a large, weathered man with a shaved head, wearing a green plaid flannel shirt.

"We are," Elias said. "Are you Mr. Ross?"

"Gunderson," the man answered. "Ross and his wife are in the dining room." He pointed toward a closed set of double doors.

Elias opened them. A handsome, dark-haired man and an attractive woman with red hair and striking green eyes were sitting at the dining room table. The man stood up and held out his hand.

"I'm Daniel Ross. You must be the detectives from Bellingham. This is my wife, Dr. Hannah Kline."

Elias shook hands and turned to Hannah. "You were the one who called us."

"Yes."

"Did one of you find the body?"

Daniel answered. "I heard a scream at 5:30 a.m. Hannah and

I ran downstairs and found Grace, the waitress, in the kitchen sobbing. I saw Mr. Nilsson in the rocking chair at the other end of the room. It was obvious from the smell, and from the livor mortis in his arms, that he was dead, and had been for a while."

"What did you do next?"

"I got Grace out of the kitchen, asked Hannah to call you, and made sure no one disturbed the scene until you had a chance to evaluate the body and make sure it was natural and not a homicide."

"Thank you. I understand you are LAPD."

"I am. I have a habit of suspecting homicide. I hope this death wasn't one and things can get back to normal here quickly."

"I'll just have a look at the body," Elias said.

Rashida opened her backpack and took out paper coveralls, booties, hoods, gloves and masks. The two of them suited up and removed the tape from the kitchen door.

They approached the body, careful not to step in the spilled liquid or squash any of the chocolates.

The man in the chair was wearing white pants and a white, short-sleeved T-shirt. His muscular arms were extensively tattooed, although the images on the lower arms were partly obscured by the purple color of the pooled blood.

Elias attempted to move the limbs. "Hard as a rock. That and his temperature should help fix the time of death."

"I don't see blood anywhere," Rashida said. "He wasn't shot, stabbed, or hit on the head, and I don't see any indication of strangulation."

The man's lids were puffy and the eyes were closed. His mouth gaped open with a swollen tongue.

"Could he have been poisoned?" Elias asked.

"Possible. While we're waiting, why don't I photograph everything and then bag the alcohol and the chocolates. We'll have to find out what he ate for dinner and take all the leftovers in the refrigerator. I don't think the doc is going to be able to tell us for sure whether it was natural without an autopsy, so we'd better treat it like a crime scene."

Rashida took a camera out of her pack and began photographing. Ordinarily, there would have been a much larger crime team, but no one had thought this death on Oriole Island would warrant it. This wasn't the first time Elias had asked Rashida to do double duty as the photographer and evidence tech. The kitchen was a small enough space so he didn't think she would have any trouble collecting the trace by herself.

"While you're doing this, and we're waiting for the doc, I'll get out of your way and interview the guests," Elias said.

Elias returned to the dining room and removed his personal protective equipment.

"We're waiting for the medical examiner, but at the moment, the odds are that the death was natural. My partner is collecting evidence, in case the autopsy shows otherwise, but there's no obvious sign of violence. I'd like to ask the two of you a few questions."

"Of course," Daniel said.

"Did you know Mr. Nilsson?"

"No. This was our first night at Alder House. We're on our honeymoon. Mr. Nilsson came out of the kitchen before dinner and introduced himself to the guests. That was the only time we saw him."

"Can you tell me what you did after dinner?" Elias addressed the question to Hannah.

"We went outside and took a walk down to the beach, to burn off some of those dessert calories. Then we returned to the hotel and went to bed."

"You didn't happen to see Mr. Nilsson when you returned, or hear any unusual noise from the kitchen?"

"Nothing," Hannah said. "We woke up when Grace screamed this morning."

Elias was writing down their answers in his notebook. "Thank you. Would you mind joining the rest of the guests in the lounge? I'd like to use the dining room to interview people. Do you happen to know where Grace is?"

Luke and Grace were sitting outside, on a pair of lawn chairs, in back of the house.

"I still can't believe it. He was a bastard but much as I disliked him, I never wished he would drop dead," Luke said. In truth, Luke hadn't felt sorry about the death.

"I wonder if Melanie will ask you to take over the kitchen," Grace said. "It would be a wonderful opportunity."

It would be, Luke thought, and if she didn't, he was out of here. He'd learned everything Scott had to teach him. Surely, he could do as well some place that wasn't so boring.

A tall, skinny man with thinning blonde hair came out the back door and headed for them.

"Are you Grace?" he asked. "Your last name?"

"Campbell."

The man held out his badge and ID. "Detective Elias Lindstrom." He turned toward Luke. "You are?"

"Luke Murray. I'm the sous-chef here." Luke could see the tension in Grace's body and he moved to put a protective arm around her.

"Would both of you mind coming inside with me? I'd like to talk to Miss Campbell in the dining room."

"Can I ask you how long it will be before I can have the kitchen back? There are hungry guests to feed," Luke said.

"A few hours," the detective replied. "As soon as the medical examiner arrives and has done his work, we'll take Mr. Nilsson's body back to Bellingham. When we're done collecting evidence, we'll release the kitchen. You'll want to do a thorough cleaning before using it again to prepare food. In the meantime, I'd like you to wait for me with the other guests in the main lounge."

Hannah sat on the sofa in the lounge, next to Daniel. Opposite her were the four writers. The Suttons were sitting together in a corner, and Gunderson was pacing up and down. No one was talking.

The dining room doors opened and Luke entered, looking uncomfortable. Hannah smiled at him and patted the seat next to her.

"Why don't you have a seat. I think we may be here for a while until the police figure things out."

Luke followed her suggestion. "The Detective is speaking to Grace now. He said I'll be able to have the kitchen back later today as soon as they've taken Scott away. They're waiting for the medical examiner to arrive."

"Does that mean we get to have dinner tonight?" Ilana asked.

"I certainly hope so," Luke said. "But I have to disinfect the kitchen first, and with only me cooking, it may be later than usual."

"I can help," Ilana said. "I don't just write culinary mysteries. I work at a restaurant in Seattle as a chef. It's just a café and the food isn't as fancy as yours but I'm a pretty good cook."

"That would be awesome," Luke said.

"Maybe after the police have finished, we could get together and come up with tonight's menu?"

Luke nodded. "I know what Scott was planning and what food we have stocked, so it shouldn't be too hard."

Hannah glanced at Daniel, who was staring past the lounge entrance to where Melanie was seated at her desk in the foyer.

There was a tense feeling in her stomach and it wasn't just the unexpected death. Daniel was hiding something from her. He'd told her Melanie had been a waitress he'd recognized from long ago, when he was stationed at Fort Lewis. Had there been something more between them that he wasn't telling her? This was not how she'd imagined their honeymoon. She hoped the medical examiner would get here soon so they could get out of here and talk.

Detective Elias watched from the foyer as the medical examiner pulled up in front of Alder House with a squeal of brakes, followed by the coroner's van. The doctor was probably feeling very put upon, thinking it was a colossal waste of his time coming all the way out to Oriole Island for some celebrity who probably had a heart attack. Carrying the bag containing his medical equipment, he climbed the steps to the front door.

"I'm glad you're here," Elias said. "Follow me."

"Let's get on with it, shall we?" He removed his personal protective equipment from his bag and suited up, following Elias into the kitchen, where Rashida was just finishing up.

"He's all yours," she said, removing her mask.

The doctor approached the body and went through his usual careful examination, testing for rigor and measuring both the body temperature and the room temperature.

Elias gave him space and waited patiently until he had completed his exam.

"So, what do you think, Doc?"

"My best estimate for the time of death is between midnight and two in the morning. He seems to have died in his chair. There is no sign of a gunshot, stabbing or strangulation. The most interesting finding is his swollen tongue and lids, and what looks like hives all over his neck, arms and chest. I won't know for sure until I finish the autopsy but it appears as if he died of an allergic reaction—anaphylaxis."

"Not poison?"

"I'd have to run the toxicology screen, but if someone has a severe allergy, the allergen is poison to them, if not to others. The coroner's van is outside. Let's get him back to Bellingham and I'll tell you more after the autopsy."

"You might want this," Rashida said to Elias. "It's his cell phone. I found it on the desk in the little office." She handed him an evidence bag.

"Thanks. I'll see if his personal doctor's information is in there. If anyone can tell us about his allergies, his internist is the guy."

The Medical Examiner left the kitchen, stripped off his paper suit, hat, booties and gloves, picked up his bag, and headed out the front door to his car. Elias watched as he motioned to the techs in the van to go in and do their job and then accelerated out of the driveway, clearly trying to make the next ferry.

9

WHILE THE TWO CORONER'S technicians extracted Nilsson's body from his chair and placed it into a black plastic body bag, Elias Lindstrom sat down on the front steps of the porch and scanned the contacts in Nilsson's phone, looking for his physician. Robert Henderson MD appeared to be the most likely contact.

"Is Dr. Henderson in? This is Detective Lindstrom of the Bellingham Police Department."

A polite receptionist put him on hold, and a moment later, the doctor was on the line.

"I'm calling about your patient, Scott Nilsson. I believe you are his personal physician," Elias said.

"Is something wrong with Scott?"

"I'm sorry to inform you that Mr. Nilsson was found dead this morning, in the kitchen at Alder House, where he worked. I wonder if you can tell me if he had any medical problems that might lead to an unexpected early death."

"I'm shocked. I don't recall anything major, but let me pull up his chart."

There was a short pause before Dr. Henderson returned to the line.

"According to my records, he was a very healthy guy for his age. He was a little overweight, and I was watching his cholesterol, but neither of those factors are unexpected in a chef."

"No heart disease?"

"None. No diabetes, hypertension, kidney disease, arthritis, lung problems. I can't imagine why he should have died suddenly at his age. Are you doing an autopsy?"

"We are. One more question. Do you know of any allergies?"

"He was quite allergic to peanuts. No other food allergies."

"Thank you, doctor. That's very helpful." Elias signed off and turned to Rashida, who had come outside to join him.

"Peanut allergy."

"Really? You think that's what killed him?"

"Don't know, but we should make sure to test for peanut protein. Let's get out of here and let the guests go about their business."

Daniel was feeling bored and agitated, sitting with the guests in the lounge, with nothing to do, while a possible crime scene investigation was going on in the next room. He was certain that the Bellingham detective would turn down any offer of help on Daniel's part. He would do the same if the situation were reversed.

Hannah had gone upstairs, returned with her Kindle, and was engrossed in a novel. He always marveled at the fact that nothing distracted her when she was reading.

None of the other guests were conversing. Each of them had spent a few minutes in the dining room with Detective Lindstrom. Some were now reading the local paper or magazines. A few were playing with their cell phones, and Samantha had brought down a laptop and was busy writing. Daniel noticed she was smiling. Perhaps she was creating a hot sex scene.

The doors to the dining room opened and Lindstrom

stepped into the lounge. Melanie left her desk and joined the guests.

"Ladies and gentlemen, thank you all for your patience and cooperation. We've removed Mr. Nilsson's body through the back door and completed our work in the kitchen. It appears that Mr. Nilsson may have died from an allergic reaction, but we won't have a final diagnosis until after the autopsy is done this afternoon. Until we are certain that no crime has been committed, we are asking you all to remain on the island. I will communicate with Miss Wells as soon as I am certain that more extensive questioning will not be necessary."

"Does this mean I can have my kitchen back? My staff needs to clean up and start the preparations for dinner tonight." Melanie said.

"It does. I apologize for any mess we made. I'll call you as soon as we have more information."

Lindstrom and his partner retrieved their packs and left by the front door, driving toward the ferry dock.

Melanie turned to the guests. "I'm so sorry you have been subjected to this tragic death and police presence. I hope to make the rest of your stay as pleasant as possible. Please go and enjoy our lovely island this afternoon and we will see you all later for our five-thirty wine and appetizers."

"Ladies," Samantha said to her group. "Why don't we rendezvous with our manuscripts on the side veranda and continue reading and critiquing?"

The three other writers followed her upstairs to their rooms.

"I'm going fishing," Gunderson announced. "If I catch anything good, I'll bring it in as a dinner contribution."

"I have some phone calls to make," Craig Sutton announced. "Come upstairs with me, Angela."

Hannah turned off her Kindle and walked over to where Daniel was standing.

"It's a beautiful day. How about a drive around the island? Let's not forget we're supposed to be on our honeymoon."

Daniel drew her to him and kissed the top of her head. "I haven't forgotten. I just got a little distracted because dead bodies seem to follow us everywhere."

"I'm going to leave my Kindle in our room and grab a jacket. Do you want yours?"

"Yes, thanks."

As Hannah ran up the stairs, Daniel turned to Melanie. "Did Scott Nilsson have any allergies?"

"Yeah. Peanuts. He was quite paranoid about them. We never had them in the kitchen and he never included peanuts or peanut oil in any recipe. He didn't want to contaminate his cooking equipment."

"No other allergies?"

"Not that I know of."

It was odd, Daniel thought. He wondered what Scott had eaten last night.

"I didn't know you were a detective," Melanie said. "I always wondered where you disappeared to after you left Tacoma."

"I moved to Los Angeles and went to the Police Academy," Daniel said.

He was surprised she had thought about him. He'd thought a good deal about her, but she hadn't been the one who had reason to feel guilty. He assumed she had just viewed him as a one night stand.

"It was handy having a detective on site this morning. If you'll excuse me, I have a kitchen to put back in order and guests to feed. Perhaps we can catch up later."

He watched Melanie walk off as Hannah descended the stairs, jackets in hand. She reached up and kissed his cheek.

"I wonder how long it will take," she said, "for that medical examiner to determine cause and manner of death."

It was late afternoon when Elias Lindstrom finally got a call from the medical examiner.

"It looks like a severe allergic reaction," the doctor said.

"Did you do a toxicology screen?" Elias asked.

"His blood alcohol was past the legal limit for driving but we didn't find any narcotics, barbiturates or anything else that would suggest poison or suicide."

"What about the stomach contents?"

"Whatever he had for dinner was long gone. The only food in his stomach was chocolate."

"No peanuts?"

"None."

"Can you have the lab test the chocolate and the cognac for peanut protein?"

"Are you thinking the truffles may have contained peanut oil and he ate them without realizing?"

"I'm thinking that someone may have deliberately given him chocolates that could kill him."

"In that case, I'll ask the lab to get it done immediately."

In the meantime, Elias thought, he'd better get his team doing research on everyone at Alder House. If this was deliberate, there were a limited number of suspects, and he needed to find out if any of them had a history with Scott Nilsson before they left the island. He'd tell them to begin with Nilsson's business partner.

Melanie breathed a sigh of relief. She and the staff had spent two hours meticulously scrubbing the kitchen until it was spotless and back to normal. Luke was busy preparing the appetizers, assisted by one of the guests who had been introduced to her earlier as Ilana, a chef from Seattle. Melanie had voiced her appreciation and offered to make Ilana's room complimentary to thank her for the help.

Opening the wine refrigerator, Melanie selected a particularly good wine for the evening. Detective Lindstrom hadn't called yet, but she was in no hurry to hear from him. She was afraid that as soon as Scott's death had been declared natural, her guests would all flee Alder House at the first opportunity, and frankly, she needed the money.

Fortunately, the restaurant was closed until the weekend, so she only had to feed the B&B guests, but she had to hire a new chef immediately or her business would disappear.

She walked through the empty lounge and toward her desk. Daniel Ross was descending the stairs. This might be the perfect time to have a chat with him.

"How are you holding up?" Daniel asked. "Is there anything I can do to help?"

"I have it under control," Melanie answered, "but I would like a word. Can we walk outside for a few minutes?"

Daniel held the door for her. It was chilly out and the sun was close to setting. Melanie shivered and decided to get right to the point.

"You disappeared after our night together, without so much as a goodbye. I had no idea where you were living."

"I never thought you would want to get in touch. It was just one night," he said. "I'm sorry if I misread the situation."

"The situation, as you call it, had some long-term consequences. You've met my son, Josh? He's your son."

Daniel's jaw dropped. "How can you be sure?"

"I'm sure because I didn't screw anyone else during the two weeks between you and my missed period. If you don't believe me, do a paternity test."

Daniel's face was grim. He didn't say anything for a long time. Melanie wondered if he was trying to figure out how to break the news to his wife, or whether to try to keep it a secret. Either way, Melanie was holding all the cards.

"What do you want from me?" he asked.

"Child support would be nice. You don't have to have

anything to do with Josh. He's managed quite nicely without a father up to now."

"Forgive me if I don't take your word for this. I'm a cop. I need hard evidence. Can we talk again tomorrow?"

"We can talk tomorrow, but I don't have much time. I need more money now and we can either work something out, or since I know where you live, I can take you to court. Your choice."

Melanie walked away.

10

THE NEXT MORNING, ELIAS LINDSTROM met with his team in the station conference room. The Chief assigned two additional detectives, in addition to Rashida, to sort out the Nilsson case. The one advantage to a celebrity death was that the lab work jumped the long queue and results came back in record time.

"It appears," Elias said, "that Scott Nilsson died from an anaphylactic reaction to peanut oil, contained in a box of truffles that he was eating after dinner. I looked up a dozen recipes for truffles and peanut oil is not an ingredient. For the moment, I am assuming that someone who knew of Nilsson's allergy deliberately created chocolates that would kill him. We are looking for a killer who knew Nilsson well enough to be aware of his allergy, who was capable of making chocolates containing the allergen, and who had a motive for his death. We also need to find out how that box of chocolates was delivered to him."

"How do we know that this wasn't an accident? Maybe there is a recipe with peanut oil and Nilsson just failed to read the ingredients?" Rashida asked.

"Certainly possible, but I don't believe in coincidence. For the moment, let's go with homicide unless we can track down those truffles and prove otherwise."

"Okay, boss. On the plus side, there are only nine guests at Alder house, plus the owner and two employees. If it really is homicide, the number of suspects is limited."

"I assume," Lindstrom said, "that we've all done our homework on the background checks. Let's set up a board with our information and see what overlaps. I'm going to call Miss Wells and let her know that we'll be coming out later this morning to do additional interviews."

Melanie made the announcement over breakfast. She couldn't have been more annoyed. She had enough trouble to sort out and didn't need the police under her feet.

"Detective Lindstrom will be here later this morning. Apparently, he isn't done questioning all of you."

"Questioning us about what?" Noel Gunderson asked. "I thought Scott died from an allergic reaction."

"He didn't say," Melanie said.

"What was he allergic to?" Angela Sutton asked.

"Peanuts," Melanie said.

"Does Lindstrom think someone forced Scott to eat a peanut butter sandwich at gunpoint?" Craig asked.

"He didn't tell me what he thinks," Melanie said. "He just requested that everyone be available."

"This is absurd. I want to go home," Angela said.

"If they're thinking someone murdered him, it certainly wasn't me," Craig said. "I stand to lose a lot of money, now that our restaurant deal bombed. I had a deposit on that space near Pike Place Market, and the other investors are not going to be happy with me."

Melanie stared at him. She had no idea what he was talking about.

"I had a great fishing day yesterday and was looking forward to another one," Noel Gunderson said. "Are you telling me I have to stay cooped up here waiting for the damn police?"

"I'm afraid so," Melanie said. "Stop giving me that look. I'm not the one responsible."

Gunderson hadn't talked to her since it happened. He probably realized that Scott's death would decimate her business unless she could replace him with another celebrity, and that wasn't going to be easy. He was probably afraid she would turn to him for financial help. Fortunately, Daniel had shown up just in time.

"I suggest you all go back to your rooms after breakfast and wait for the police. They should be here soon," Melanie said.

The writer's group retreated to Samantha's room, which was the largest and offered privacy as well as comfort. Samantha and Kylie sank into the armchairs flanking the fireplace. Vanessa sat on the window seat and Ilana propped herself up on Samantha's queen sized bed.

"Well," Samantha said. "Who imagined we'd have a real live murder mystery for Ilana to solve?" Although she hoped the medical examiner would decide it was a heart attack.

"In my mysteries, the cops are always dumb and the brilliant chef figures out who did it. I'm not sure these cops will fit into my plotline," Ilana said.

"Are you going to tell us who did it?" Vanessa asked.

"And spoil the fun?"

Vanessa squealed. "Do you *know*?!"

"Haven't a clue. The truth is, I never figure out who did it until I'm more than halfway through. Hopefully you'll figure it out after I do."

"Seriously, a chef has been murdered. Do you think the police suspect one of us?" Kylie asked.

"Why would they?" Samantha said. "We've been together non-stop since we arrived, except for when we were asleep. None of us had the opportunity to spike Scott Nilsson's dinner with peanut butter."

"They may be looking for someone who knew him before he came here and had a motive to kill him. If they do their homework, they might make some connections," Ilana replied.

"Even if they do discover a connection, they still have to establish a motive and obtain enough evidence to convict their suspect," Samantha declared. "I suggest we stop worrying about it and get to work. It's Vanessa's turn to read. I'm looking forward to your next chapter." Samantha had been enjoying mentoring the young writer.

Vanessa opened her briefcase and took out a manuscript. "I've been struggling with this chapter for months, but I've finally gotten the first draft done. It's about my sister Evelyn. She died of a drug overdose when I was a teenager. It's been so painful to write about it."

"I hope you find it therapeutic to read out loud," Samantha said. "We're all here to support you, and we're listening. Why don't we continue this on the porch and take advantage of the lovely weather?"

Hannah sat on the bed and watched Daniel pace between the window and the fireplace.

"You've been agitated since last night," she said. "This death doesn't have anything to do with us and I refuse to let it spoil our honeymoon. Are you having trouble watching another police department investigate a case when you aren't in charge?"

Daniel stopped pacing and sat down in one of the armchairs. "It's not that. I learned something last night that I'm having trouble dealing with and I don't know how to tell you."

"I'm listening, sweetheart. Just say it."

Daniel took a deep breath and made eye contact. "Remember I told you that I'd known Melanie Wells briefly when I was in the military, that she was a waitress at a bar I went to during off hours?"

"I remember."

"What I didn't tell you was that she and I had a one night stand, just before I was decommissioned and moved to Los Angeles."

"Weren't you married to Annie when you were in the Army?"

"Yeah, I was, and I can't tell you how guilty I felt about it afterwards."

Hannah didn't know what to say. She had never imagined finding out, on her honeymoon that her brand new husband had cheated on his first wife. She'd never thought of Daniel as that kind of a guy. Had he cheated on her while they lived together? Could she trust him not to cheat now that they were married? The silence between them grew.

"Why are you telling me this now?" Hannah asked.

"Because there's more. Last night, Melanie told me that I'm the father of her son. She wants child support and suggested I take a paternity test if I don't believe her."

"Do you believe her?" Hannah asked.

"I don't know what to believe and I don't know what to do." He stared at her, waiting, as if she could magically produce the right answer.

Hannah was speechless.

Elias Lindstrom drove his car up the ramp to the ferry. Rashida sat next to him in the passenger seat.

"So," she said, "have you decided who to talk to first once we get there?"

Elias put the car in park, turned off the engine, and motioned for her to get out and take the stairs to the deck. Once they had a private spot, he turned to her.

"I think our first priority should be finding out where those chocolates came from. Did they arrive by mail or UPS, or did someone bring them and just leave them in the kitchen?"

"We also need to consider who would be able to make truffles. We have three individuals with culinary training. Luke Murray, naturally but there are two other guests, both in that writing group, who are good possibilities. Kylie Evans and her husband are in the restaurant business and she trained at the Culinary Institute at the same time that Nilsson did. Ilana Flores worked at a very expensive Seattle restaurant during the time that Nilsson was the head chef. Either or both of them might have a motive for murder," Rashida said.

"Agreed. Those individuals should be our top priority. We also need to get everyone's fingerprints. Perhaps the lab will find prints on the box or on the remaining chocolates."

Rashida shrugged. "I'm not sure that will be helpful. Any one of them could have touched the box while reaching for a candy. If I were the perp, I'd wear gloves."

"Let's just hope that our killer isn't as smart as you are."

Melanie was seated at her desk when the two detectives arrived. She didn't look any too pleased to see them. Elias hoped she would be cooperative.

"So, how can I help you?" she said. "Do you know yet how Scott died?"

"He died from an allergic reaction," Elias said. "You can help by telling me about that box of chocolates that was in the kitchen. Where did it come from?"

"Truthfully, I have no idea," Melanie said. "I did notice it when I went to the kitchen to say goodnight, but I don't know who brought it in."

"Could it have arrived by mail or UPS?" Rashida asked.

"Not that I remember. I'm the one who picks up the mail, and the UPS guy usually comes in and gives me any packages."

"Do you cook?" Elias asked.

"Me? I eat. Scott cooked. When left to my own devices, I microwave frozen dinners."

"Where is the rest of your staff?"

"Luke's in the kitchen. Grace is upstairs making beds."

"Thanks," Elias said. He and Rashida proceeded to the kitchen.

They found Luke chopping salad vegetables.

"May we have a word?" Elias said. He waited until he had Luke's attention.

Luke set aside his knife and looked up.

"I'm wondering about that box of chocolates that was in the kitchen. Where did it come from?"

"It was a gift from a grateful guest. I found it Monday morning on the counter with a note that said "Thanks for one of the best meals of my life."

"Was the note signed?" Rashida asked.

"Not that I remember. The chocolates looked homemade and they were delicious. Each one was flavored with a different liqueur."

"Did you try some?"

"Quite a few, actually. We all did."

"Do you still have the note?" Lindstrom asked.

"I don't think so. It's probably in the paper recycling on the back porch."

"Do you have any idea how the chocolate box got here? Was it delivered by mail perhaps?"

Luke pursed his lips and thought for a while. "It couldn't have been. There's no mail on Sunday, and the Monday mail doesn't arrive until the afternoon. Someone must have come in and left it when the kitchen was empty."

"And when is the kitchen empty?"

"We start cooking at six-thirty in the morning, and the kitchen is pretty much used continuously until we leave after dinner."

"So you're suggesting that someone must have left the chocolates there late Sunday night," Rashida said.

"I guess so."

"Could anyone from outside enter the B&B after hours and drop off a box?" Elias asked.

"We lock the house when the staff leaves. Scott was usually the last person out of here and he took care of both the front and back doors."

"Who has keys?"

"Melanie does, I do and Grace has one. Scott did as well."

"What's going to happen to your job now that Scott is gone?" Rashida asked. "Are you going to take over as chef?"

"I have no idea. Miss Wells hasn't said anything, but I'll tell you this. If she doesn't promote me to chef, I'm leaving. There are plenty of opportunities for someone with my training elsewhere."

"Can you recall when the rest of the staff left the B&B on Sunday night?"

"Miss Wells left early. She always does on Sunday. She likes to spend time with her kid. Grace and I always leave together after the breakfast table is set, around nine o'clock."

"And Nilsson?"

"He was in his office when we left."

"Thank you. We have to take your fingerprints for elimination purposes, and then we'll leave you to your lettuce."

11

MELANIE WAS STILL AT HER DESK WHEN Elias emerged from the kitchen. What did he want from her now?

"I'd like to look at your registration records," he said. "I want to know which of your guests were staying here on Sunday night."

Melanie pulled up the information and turned the computer screen toward the detective.

"The four women arrived on Friday, as did Mr. Gunderson. The Suttons and the Ross couple checked in Monday afternoon."

"Who else stayed here on Sunday?" he asked.

Melanie scrolled down to two other names. "They checked out at noon."

"Would you mind telling me what you did on Sunday night?" the detective asked.

Was he really suspecting her of murdering Scott? "I went home early, just after the guests sat down to dinner, and spent the evening with Josh, my son."

"Did you return to the B&B at all that night?"

"Why would I?" She'd been occupied until quite late,

enjoying Noel Gunderson, but no need for the nosy detective to find out about that.

"I assume you and Mr. Nilsson had a partnership agreement. What happens to his share of the business after his death?"

"It reverts to me, but without Scott there won't be much business unless I can find another chef of his caliber."

"What was the arrangement if you died first?"

"My son would have inherited my share with Scott as the executor until Josh turned 21."

"Were you aware that Scott Nilsson was about to leave you?"

"What?"

"When I interviewed Mr. Sutton yesterday, he mentioned that he and Mr. Nilsson were about to sign a contract to open a Nilsson's restaurant in Seattle and to franchise in other cities as well. Nilsson planned to hire a substitute chef to take over here."

"I don't believe you."

"It's true. Whether Scott was alive or dead, you would be working with a substitute chef, only now the whole business and all its profits are yours."

"Are you accusing me of something?"

"Not yet," Elias said, "but I am pointing out that you might have had a motive for Nilsson's death. I hope you don't mind, but we're going to need your fingerprints."

Elias touched base with Rashida on the back porch. She was wearing latex gloves and stuffing all the paper from the recycling bin into evidence bags.

"We can sort this later, when we get back to the station," she said.

"What did you learn?" he asked.

"Grace corroborated what Luke Murray told us. She ate the chocolate and claims not to have known that Scott Nilsson was allergic to peanuts. I can't see that she had anything to gain by his death. She may find herself out of a job."

"Miss Wells seemed surprised when I told her about Scott's restaurant deal with Craig Sutton, but she could have been acting. If she knew, she certainly had a motive."

"If it was murder," Rashida said, "the method was clever. The killer could get rid of Nilsson and not worry that the tainted chocolate would affect anyone else. It's much easier than trying to slip strychnine into just one bowl of soup."

"I think we can rule out the two couples who arrived on Monday," Elias said. "The Suttons had a great deal to gain with Scott alive, and the detective and his wife have no connection to him that we've been able to uncover. I think we should move on to Gunderson."

They found Noel Gunderson on the front porch, seated on an Adirondack chair.

"Let's get this over with," he said. "You're interfering with my fishing."

"So sorry," Rashida said. "Of course, your fishing is so much more important than our murder investigation." The two detectives pulled over chairs and flanked Gunderson on both sides.

Elias leaned forward. He was pissed. "Let's get one thing straight. You're staying on this island until I give you permission to leave. You are a person of interest."

Gunderson's face turned red. Elias watched the process as the man struggled between losing his temper and coming to terms with being outmatched.

"Fine. What do you want to know? Should I call my lawyer?"

"That's up to you. Right now, you aren't a suspect. You are

just helping us with our investigation. If you'd prefer to stay here until your lawyer can arrive from Bellingham or Seattle, we'll question someone else."

"But," Rashida added, "no fishing until after you answer our questions."

"Shit," Gunderson said. "I have nothing to hide. Go ahead."

"How long and how well did you know Scott Nilsson?" Elias asked.

"I've been coming to Alder House for years to fish. I met Nilsson when he arrived three years ago. We weren't friends, but he was always happy to cook my catch for me."

"Did you like him?"

Gunderson shrugged. "I liked his cooking. He wasn't a friendly guy. Big ego and bossy. The staff was afraid of him."

"Did you ever witness any unpleasant interactions between Nilsson and his staff?"

"I'd hear him yelling at them, never when meals were being served, but in the middle of the day when they were doing the preps for the restaurant."

"What about his relationship with Miss Wells?" Rashida asked. "Did they get along?"

"They were living together at her house when he first came, but that didn't last long. He bought his own place as soon as the restaurant became successful. I think he still stops by for a quickie, but I don't have the impression that it's a great love affair."

"Did you ever see them fight?" Elias asked. This was interesting new information.

"Not in front of me."

"I understand you arrived last Friday. Can you tell me how you spent Sunday afternoon and night?"

"Went fishing, had dinner, took a walk, went to bed. It's what I do every day I'm here."

"You didn't, by any chance, drop off a gift for Scott in the kitchen Sunday night?"

"No. Why would I give him a gift?"

"In appreciation of the best meal you ever ate?" Elias suggested.

Gunderson just looked puzzled.

"Can anyone else vouch for your movements Sunday night?" Rashida asked.

"Do I need some sort of alibi? Scott Nilsson was alive all day Monday," Gunderson said. "I don't understand what you're getting at."

"You don't need to understand. You just need to answer my question."

"If you want an alibi, I've got one for both Sunday and Monday night. I was in bed with Melanie Wells. That's how I spend all my nights when I'm here."

Rashida raised her eyebrows. "Did Scott Nilsson know about your relationship with his partner?"

"I don't think he knew, but he wouldn't have given a shit if he had."

"So, what time did you leave Miss Wells to return to your room?"

"I didn't look at my watch, but I split before her kid wakes up. Could have been two, maybe three."

"When you returned to Alder House on Sunday night did you see or hear anyone else?" Rashida asked.

"Quiet as a tomb."

"All right," Elias said. "You can go fishing. Just don't leave the island until I say you can."

Next he needed to find the four ladies.

The writer's group was seated at an outdoor table on the side veranda, taking advantage of the sun.

"You must feel so angry and sad at the same time,"

Samantha said. "No wonder it was difficult for you to write about it."

They'd all had difficult moments in their lives. One of the strengths of their group had been their ability to share them with one another through their writing.

Vanessa blotted her eyes with a tissue. "Thanks for being so supportive. I haven't been able to talk to anyone about this since Evelyn died. I've been dreaming for years about getting my revenge on the bastard who got her hooked on Oxycontin."

"They say revenge is best served cold," Kylie said.

Vanessa flushed. Samantha wondered what she was thinking. Then she noticed the two detectives rounding the corner of the house.

"Ladies," Elias said. "We'd like to have a word with each of you alone. Miss Flores, would you come inside with me please? Mrs. Evans, would you accompany Detective James?"

Ilana and Kylie rose from their chairs, gathered their papers, and followed the detectives into the house.

Samantha chewed her bottom lip. She wondered why the detectives were back and what they were planning to ask her.

Ilana's heart was beating fast. If the detectives were here, surely that meant Scott Nilsson's death wasn't natural. Were they suspecting her? She hugged her novel to her chest, and took a seat in one of the armchairs in the empty lounge.

Elias smiled at her, which did nothing to put her at ease. "Miss Flores, I understand that you are also a chef."

"Yes, that's right."

"Do you cook the same kind of food as Mr. Nilsson?"

"Not at all. I work in a Mexican cafe and make things like enchiladas and burritos."

"Do you know how to make truffles?" he asked.

"I don't do desserts. Making chocolate confections is a specialty. There are people who do nothing but create candies."

"I see. I understand that you worked at Mon Cher at the time Mr. Nilsson was the chef. Did you know him well?"

Ilana tensed. Of course, they would have found out she'd worked with Scott. They were the police after all.

"Why are you asking me all these questions? I thought Mr. Nilsson died a perfectly natural death."

"There is some ambiguity about that. I'm trying to get a more complete picture of the man," Elias answered. "Did you know him well?"

"I was one of six sous-chefs at Mon Cher. I doubt Nilsson could tell us apart. He never spoke personally to any of us."

"It sounds as if he wasn't well liked," Elias said.

"He was a brilliant chef. I doubt he cared whether he was liked."

"Why did you leave Mon Cher? According to their records, you left a year before he did."

"I got an offer to be head chef at a Mexican restaurant that was owned by a friend of my family. I knew I'd never be the chef at Mon Cher. It was time to move on."

Time to get away from Nilsson's verbal and physical abuse. The employees all hated him but his meals kept the customers packing the restaurant. Ilana couldn't wait to escape.

"I understand your group arrived here on Sunday afternoon. Is that correct?"

"Yes."

"Tell me exactly what you all did, and where you were on Sunday night."

Ilana's eyebrows scrunched up as she tried to remember. "We got here in the late afternoon, unpacked, met downstairs for wine and appetizers, and then had dinner. After dinner, we convened in Samantha's room to go over the retreat schedule for the week."

"What did you do after that?"

"I went back to my room and went to bed."

"At what time?"

"I think it was around eleven."

"Did you see or hear anything unusual during the night?"

"Like what?"

"Doors opening or closing, footsteps?"

"I sleep like the dead, Detective. There could have been a rap concert going on outside and I wouldn't have heard it."

"What time did you get up?"

"Seven-thirty. We all met for breakfast at eight."

"Thank you, Miss Flores. I'll let you know if I have any more questions."

Leaving Ilana Flores, Elias joined Rashida in the dining room where she and Kylie were waiting for him. Kylie looked self-assured in her designer jeans and leather jacket, having seated herself comfortably at the head of the table.

"What can I do for you detectives?" she asked.

Elias wanted to wipe that confident smile off her face. "I understand you trained at the Culinary Institute at the same time as Scott Nilsson. How well did you know him?"

Kylie raised her eyebrows just a fraction. "Scott was the star of the class, quite creative and brilliant when it came to cuisine. He didn't mix much with the hoi polloi."

"So, not well?"

Kylie shrugged. "Scott always wanted to be a great chef. I just wanted to know enough about cooking so that I could go into restaurant management. I had no desire to be chopping vegetables in the kitchen."

"I can understand that. Did you get your wish?"

"I married George Evans. Our company has a very large chain of successful restaurants. Why am I here?"

"We have some concerns about Scott's death. Tell me, when

you studied at the Culinary Institute, did they teach you how to make truffles?" Elias asked.

He watched her face and body language as she answered. It told him nothing. The woman was a master of self-control.

"That's an advanced elective course in the dessert and pastry track, so no."

"Tell me what you did when you got here on Sunday."

"Unpacked, had a few glasses of wine, went to dinner and then met with my group to discuss our plans for the week."

"Were you all together after dinner?"

"Yes."

"What time did the meeting break up?"

"I'm not sure, probably around ten-thirty or eleven."

"Where did you go after that?"

"To bed."

"Did everyone go to bed?"

"I didn't follow them all to their rooms, but I assume so."

"Did you see or hear anything unusual during the night?"

"I take an Ambien to go to sleep, Detective. I hear nothing."

Elias rose and motioned for Rashida to follow him. "That will be all for now. Thank you, Mrs. Evans."

Two down, Elias thought, and two to go. Maybe they'd learn something substantial when they interviewed Samantha. She seemed to be the leader of this little group.

12

Samantha and Vanessa were still seated in the Adirondack chairs on the side porch when the two detectives went looking for them. They escorted Samantha to the lounge and asked Vanessa to wait.

"I gather, since you're back here asking questions, there's something fishy about Mr. Nilsson's death," Samantha said as she seated herself, trying to control her anxiety about being interviewed by the police.

"You're correct, Dr. Hunter," Elias said.

Samantha sighed. "I see you've tracked down my real name. I do keep my dual identity a closely guarded secret from both my readers and my academic colleagues. I rely on your discretion, Detective Lindstrom. If it got out that I write romance novels, it would undermine my credibility as a serious historian."

"At the moment, I see no need to go public with your information. I do have some additional questions. Can you give me a timeline of everything you and your group did after your arrival Sunday afternoon?"

"That's easy. We checked in around three in the afternoon, got together at five-thirty for wine and appetizers, dined and then met in my room after dinner to plan our week. When we do these retreats, we designate certain times for writing, and specific hours to read and give one another feedback on what has been written. At this point, we are all very familiar with one another's work and style."

"When did you end the meeting?"

"I'm not exactly sure, but I think it was between eleven and twelve. We'd had a long day and everyone wanted to get some sleep."

"Did you hear or see anything unusual during the night?"

"As a matter of fact, I did. I'm not a sound sleeper and I get up several times a night to empty my bladder. One of those times, I did hear footsteps and a door closing nearby. The rest of my group are in the east wing so it must have been one of the other guests. I don't know who occupies which room."

"What time was that?" Elias asked.

Samantha shook her head. "All I can tell you is that it was the last time I got up before morning. It could have been as late as four or five a.m."

"How well did you know Scott Nilsson?"

"Not at all. I met him Sunday night briefly, for the first time."

"You teach at the University of Chicago. Scott Nilsson grew up and lived in Chicago until he moved to New York State to study at the Culinary Institute. Are you sure you never met him?"

"Really, Detective. Chicago is a very big city. Do you know everyone in Bellingham?" She raised her eyebrows and gave him the look she used to quell unruly students.

"Do you cook, Dr. Hunter? Know how to make truffles, perhaps?" Elias asked.

"I order in and reheat. And no, I've never made truffles."

"Do any of your fellow writers have a previous relationship with Scott Nilsson?"

"I believe Ilana worked with him at some restaurant in Seattle, years ago. I don't know if anyone else was acquainted with him."

If the police had uncovered her identity as Mildred Hunter, they probably already knew about Ilana.

"Thank you, Dr. Hunter. That will be all for the moment."

The two detectives returned to the porch and pulled up two more chairs so they could sit and face Vanessa.

"This won't take long Miss Brooks." Elias could tell that she was tense and he smiled to put her at ease. "I just need a summary of your activities on Sunday night."

Vanessa clasped her hands together and pursed her lips as if she was trying hard to remember. "We had just arrived. I unpacked and changed, and then joined the other guests for appetizers and dinner. It was an excellent meal."

"And after dinner?" Elias prodded.

"We went to Samantha's room and talked for a while. Then I went to bed."

"Did you see or hear anything unusual after you returned to your room?"

She gave him a puzzled look. "Not really. I went right to sleep."

"What do you do for a living Miss Brooks?" Elias noticed her body relaxing. This was a question to which she knew the right answer.

"I manage a boutique hotel in Seattle."

"Have you ever had a professional or personal interaction with Scott Nilsson?"

Elias watched as her body tensed again.

"I never met him. He made an announcement at dinner Sunday night. That was the first time I'd set eyes on him."

"Thank you," Elias said. "Just one more question. Do you happen to know how to make truffles?"

Vanessa smiled at him. "I make it a point not to know how to cook anything fattening, Detective."

"That will be all for now," Elias said.

Vanessa picked up her papers and disappeared into the house.

Elias turned to Rashida. "What do you think?"

"I think she was much more on edge than I expected. We didn't find any place where her background overlapped Nilsson's, but my instincts tell me she's hiding something."

"I agree. Let's go speak to Melanie Wells again. It seems she didn't tell us everything either."

"No one tells the police everything," Rashida muttered.

Melanie looked up from her desk to see the two detectives returning. Were they ever going to leave her alone? She had enough problems to deal with.

"Back again?" she asked.

"Afraid so. We'd like to know who occupies the rooms in the West wing," Lindstrom said.

Melanie turned to her computer. "Samantha Allen is in the end room. Mr. Gunderson, and Mr. and Mrs. Sutton occupy the two adjacent rooms."

"Mr. Gunderson tells me that he spent part of Sunday and Monday night in your bed. Can you confirm that?"

"What has my sex life got to do with any of this?" Melanie said. She was pissed at Noel and his big mouth.

"I'm not interested in your sex life," Lindstrom said. "I just want to know what time Mr. Gunderson left your home Sunday night."

Melanie shrugged. "I can't tell you. He was gone when I woke up at seven. He always makes it a point to leave before Josh wakes."

"We understand you had a relationship with Mr. Nilsson

that was more than business," Rashida said. "You failed to mention that."

"You didn't ask," Melanie said. "Scott and I were partners with benefits. We occasionally had sex but we weren't exclusive."

"When was the last time you slept with him?" Lindstrom asked.

Melanie shrugged. "I don't recall. It was a few weeks ago. As I said, occasional."

"Are either of those two men the father of your son?" Rashida asked.

"No."

"Who is his father?"

Melanie smiled. She felt no hesitation about sharing that piece of information with the police.

"Detective Daniel Ross," she said.

Daniel was seated on a log on the beach, a perch to which he had retreated after Hannah had asked him to go for a walk and leave her alone, so she could think about what he'd just told her. Her face had been blank. He couldn't tell if she was devastated, furious, ready to leave him or all of the above. He just knew that somehow, he'd blundered badly and may have destroyed their marriage before it even had a chance to begin.

He wondered which aspect of his confession had upset her the most; the fact that he'd cheated on Annie, that he hadn't told her the full truth about Melanie, or that he might have an illegitimate son. He thought about how he might feel if the situation was reversed.

A brisk breeze blew in over the water and he shivered. Time to go inside. He'd been sitting on the beach for over an hour. Hannah might not be ready to see him yet, but at least he could sit in the lounge and have a hot tea.

As he got up, he noticed the two detectives walking toward him. They paused and waited as he approached the house.

"A word, Mr. Ross," Detective Lindstrom said.

"Certainly. Do you mind if we talk inside? It's getting chilly out here."

Daniel led the way into the empty lounge, made himself a mug of chai, and sat down on one of the armchairs. The two detectives sat opposite him.

"Have you determined the cause and manner of death yet?" Daniel asked, cupping his hands around the warm mug.

"The cause was an anaphylactic reaction to peanuts contained in the truffles Mr. Nilsson ate. We are currently investigating whether the truffles were given to him in a deliberate attempt to commit murder."

"I see. How can I help?"

"We have a few more questions for you, Mr. Ross," Elias Lindstrom said.

Daniel noticed Lindstrom was pointedly not addressing him as Detective. This was not a collegial conversation.

"You told us that you met Scott Nilsson for the first time prior to Monday night's dinner. You didn't mention that you were not only acquainted with Melanie Wells, but that you were the father of her child."

So that was it. Melanie must have told them. There wasn't any reason other than spitefulness to do so. It was hardly related to Scott's death. She must want him off balance.

"I hadn't seen or heard from Miss Wells in fifteen years, and until yesterday I had no idea she had a son, much less that she believed I was the father."

"Do you think she lied to you?"

"I think she believes what she told me. I need to see the evidence before I can believe it."

"Paternity tests don't lie," Detective James said. "Did she offer you one?"

"She did."

"Did you know that Melanie Wells owned Alder House when you decided to come here?" Lindstrom asked.

"Of course not. I'm on my honeymoon. Why would I want my new wife to meet a very old former sexual partner?"

"How long were you and Miss Wells a couple?" Lindstrom asked.

"We were never a couple. We had a one night stand when I was stationed at Fort Lewis, just before the end of my tour. I didn't recognize her when I got here. I only remembered who she was when she mentioned her name and it rang a bell."

"What does she want?" Rashida asked.

"Money."

"Are you going to give it to her?"

"You're putting the cart before the horse. First I need to know if her son really is my son." Daniel hoped with all his heart that the paternity test would be negative. He wanted Hannah's baby, their baby, not some teenage boy he hadn't known existed.

"Did she want you to dump your wife and stay here with her? She owns a lucrative business. Might be much nicer than corralling scum in Los Angeles. Now that Scott's dead, she owns it all."

"You'll have to ask her what she wants. All I want is to resolve this situation quickly and go home with Hannah."

"Have you told your new bride about this?" Lindstrom asked.

"Yes."

"What did she say?"

"She's still processing it. Not the kind of thing you expect to learn on your honeymoon."

"How do we know you're telling the truth? Maybe you and Melanie conspired together to murder her partner, so you three could be a family, and she would inherit Nilsson's half of the business."

"Melanie needs a chef to run this business, not a homicide

detective who can't cook anything but French toast. If you're implying that I had anything to do with Scott Nilsson's death, I won't talk to you further without an attorney present," Daniel said.

"We'll need to talk to your wife. Where is she?"

"I think she's still in our room."

"Rashida, would you run upstairs and ask Mrs. Ross to join us?"

Hannah was lying on the queen-sized bed, her face buried in the damp pillow. She'd finally stopped crying but she still felt as if a brick was pressing on her chest. Had she just made the biggest mistake of her life? Had her judgment been so badly flawed, that she'd failed to recognize a cheater in their two years together?

There was a knock on her door. "Mrs. Ross, are you there? It's Detective Rashida James."

Hannah rolled over. "What?"

"We'd like a few words with you. Can you come downstairs?"

"I was taking a nap. Give me a few minutes." She forced herself to sit on the edge of the bed and then dragged herself into the bathroom. Her eyes were bloodshot and puffy with crying. Her hair was a mess and her eyelashes were clumped together with tears. What possible questions could the detectives have for her?

She washed her face in cold water and took out her makeup. Foundation, blush, lipstick, eyeliner and mascara took care of everything except the bloodshot eyes. She'd have to remember to keep her lids partly closed. No way was she going to allow them to see she'd been crying. She brushed her hair and twisted it into a bun, anchoring it firmly with large pins. Her T shirt was wrinkled, so she changed to a fresh one and put on her sneakers. Slipping the key into her jeans pocket, she left the room.

The two detectives were waiting for her in the lounge. Daniel was nowhere to be seen.

"Have a seat, Mrs. Ross," Detective Lindstrom said, closing the door to the room.

"It's Dr. Kline," Hannah said. She noticed a smile tugging at the corners of Detective James's mouth. Hannah chose an armchair close to the fireplace.

"Just a few questions, Doctor," he said. "Were you aware that your husband was an old friend of Melanie Wells?"

"No." Hannah saw no need to elaborate. This was a situation in which one word answers were the best. Where was he going with this?

"Did you know that your husband was the father of Miss Wells' son?"

"I know that she believes he is." Hannah kept her face an expressionless blank.

"Did your husband communicate with Miss Wells prior to your trip to Oriole Island?"

"I don't know."

"Did you see or hear them converse with one another after you arrived?"

"We both talked to her when we checked in. I didn't witness any other conversation."

"Did your husband know Scott Nilsson prior to your arrival at Oriole."

"No."

"Did you?"

"No."

The two detectives exchanged a look. Detective James took over.

"How did you feel when your husband told you he had fathered Miss Wells' son?" she asked.

That wasn't what Daniel had told her and she wouldn't believe it until there was genetic evidence.

"I don't see what any of this has to do with Scott Nilsson's death. Are you finished questioning me?"

"For now," Lindstrom said.

Hannah got up, left the lounge without a backward glance, and went upstairs.

"Cool customer," Elias commented. It had been a most unsatisfactory interview.

"Were you hoping for an angry, hysterical wife?" Rashida asked.

"She could have been more forthcoming."

"She's very smart, she's married to a cop and she clearly knows that the less said, the better. She's obviously been crying."

"How can you tell?"

"Her eyes are bloodshot and her makeup is perfect. She told me she'd been taking a nap. She went to a good deal of trouble to appear composed before she came downstairs."

"Women..." Elias muttered. "I would like to be a fly on the wall when she sees her husband."

13

WHEN HANNAH OPENED THE DOOR TO their room, she found Daniel seated on the bed. He must have gone upstairs while she was speaking to the detectives.

"Hannah, I'm so sorry. This wasn't how I'd imagined our honeymoon."

"Me either. What exactly are you sorry for?"

"For Melanie, the murder, the detectives, the questioning, all of it."

Hannah sat down in one of the armchairs, digging her fingers into the plush blue velvet. "Have you decided what you're going to do about Melanie Wells?"

"I think so. There is only one right thing to do. I'm going to take Melanie up on her offer of a paternity test, and if she's telling the truth, I'm going to pay her child support and make sure there's enough money for her son's education."

Hannah felt a small pang of relief. At least Daniel's conscience was in working order. "Do you think it's true?"

"It could be, but I was hardly her only sexual partner. She was experienced and she had a great many fans among the enlisted men who patronized that bar. I need to act on the basis of evidence."

"You cheated on Annie. How could you?" More than anything, this was what was eating at her.

"It was a big mistake. We'd been apart for months and whenever we talked, we argued. I felt as if the marriage was coming apart and I made a stupid, impulsive decision that I regretted afterwards. Believe me Hannah, it was the only time, and I would never cheat on you."

She didn't know what to say to that because she wasn't sure she believed him.

"The detectives asked me if I knew that you were the father of Melanie's son and if the two of you had communicated before we came here. What was that about?"

"Melanie must have told them. I can't think why except as a way of striking out at me. Unfortunately, I'm now a suspect."

"What? That's absurd." If there was one thing Hannah was sure of, it was that Daniel had nothing to do with Scott Nilsson's death.

"Detective Lindstrom has a theory. Scott Nilsson died from a severe allergic reaction to peanuts, which were apparently contained in a box of truffles. He suggested that Melanie and I conspired to kill him so that she would inherit his half of the business, and I could quit the LAPD, move up here and live with her."

"Taking over the kitchen no doubt. Your scrambled eggs would certainly rate a Michelin star."

Daniel grinned. "You forgot my pancakes. Unfortunately, I do think that I am seriously being considered a murder suspect."

Hannah sighed. She hadn't decided whether or not she could forgive him, but having Daniel in jail was not an option.

"Then I guess you and I are going to have to solve this crime ourselves."

Daniel got up from the bed and took his backpack out of the closet. It was clear that Hannah was still upset, but at least she was talking to him. He removed his laptop from the bag.

"You brought your computer on our honeymoon?"

"I thought we might want to stream a movie. Did you bring yours?"

"I brought an iPad so we could Skype with Zoe. Do you need the password for the internet?"

"Yes, please."

Hannah opened the drawer of the bedside table and removed a card with information, handing it to Daniel. "What do you think we should do first? Did Lindstrom tell you anything useful?"

"Peanuts in the truffles is all I know. He certainly isn't going to share any of the forensics or background information he's already obtained, or anything he learned from his interviews."

"Why does he think it's murder, not a careless accident?"

"He didn't say, but I'd venture to guess that all the truffles contained peanuts in a form that wasn't obvious."

"You mean the chocolate wasn't rolled in chopped nuts so you could see it?"

"That's my assumption. It's actually a clever murder method if you want to kill someone with a severe nut allergy. Just add peanut oil or finely chopped nut dust to a food that your victim assumes is safe to eat."

"Unlike arsenic, you don't have to worry that an innocent person will accidentally ingest it. It would be quite specific," Hannah said. "So we need to find someone with a strong motive and some culinary skill."

"That's what I think."

As Daniel plugged in his computer and connected it to the WiFi, there was a tentative knock at the door. "Who is it?"

"It's Grace, Mr. Ross. Would you like me to make up the bed and clean the room?"

Hannah went to open the door. "Let's see what I can find out from her," she whispered to Daniel.

"Come in, Grace." Grace took an armful of clean sheets and towels from her housekeeping cart and followed Hannah inside. She folded back the comforter and began to strip the bed.

"Daniel and I were just talking about the detectives," Hannah said. "Do you know why they're back?"

Grace plumped up the down pillows and put on fresh pillowcases. "Not really. No one tells me anything."

"Detective Lindstrom said something about truffles. Any idea what he was talking about?"

Grace looked up as she smoothed the sheets. "Oh, those. They were a gift from a guest. I noticed them Monday morning in the kitchen."

"Do you know which guest?"

"It's a mystery. There was a note thanking Scott for a fabulous meal but it was unsigned. The truffles were delicious though. They were made with different liquor flavors. We all had some."

"Did Scott Nilsson have any?"

"I didn't see him eat any during dinner but he must have eaten some later, don't you think? I saw the box on the floor and the chocolates scattered near his body." Grace paused and used the back of her hand to wipe a tear from her eye.

"I can see how upset you are," Hannah said. "Let me give you a hand."

She took hold of the other side of the comforter and helped Grace straighten it, after which Grace retreated to the bathroom to replace the towels and clean the fixtures.

Daniel gave Hannah a thumbs up sign. Her interrogation technique was excellent.

"I'm going to go downstairs and have a few words with Melanie. I think you might be able to get Grace to give you more information if you're alone with her."

"What are you going to say to Melanie?"

"I'm going to agree to that paternity test," he said.

Melanie was sitting at the front desk, her chin resting on her hands, trying to decide what to do next, when she heard Daniel coming down the stairs. Finally. She'd wondered how long it would take him to agree to her demands.

He stood in front of her desk and she looked up at him. "So Daniel, have you had a chance to process my information?"

"I have."

"And?"

"And I think the next step is a paternity test. You offered it and I'm taking you up on your offer. If it shows that I truly am your son's father, I will take responsibility."

"I assumed you'd insist on a test, so I purchased one online after you made your reservation." She opened the bottom drawer of her desk and removed a cardboard box. "All you have to do is swab your cheek and mail the test tube to the lab. I've already gotten a witnessed sample from Josh. We should have the results in two or three days if we send it by FedEx."

Opening the carton, she removed the test package and handed it to him. "Naturally, I want this result to be legal in court, so you'll also have to collect the swab in the presence of a witness and have the paperwork signed."

"Chain of custody, I assume," he said.

"Naturally, and your witness can't be your wife. She has a vested interest in a negative test."

"No problem. I'll collect it right now. We can ask one of the detectives to witness it, since you went to the trouble of telling them I fathered your son. Why did you do that, by the way?"

"Just wanted to keep you on your toes," Melanie said. Every time she saw him, she felt angrier.

"It's backfired on you. Now Detective Lindstrom is convinced that you and I plotted together to kill your partner."

"To what end? Why would I want to kill the goose who was laying the golden egg around here?" He couldn't be serious. She was the one with the most to lose from Scott's death.

"Maybe the egg was rotten," Daniel suggested. "Let's go find the detectives. I want to get this over with." Besides, he needed to return to their room and get his investigation underway.

Grace emerged from the bathroom, hugging the moist towels to her chest.

"How are you holding up, Grace?" Hannah asked. "I know how horrible it feels to find a body. It happened once to me." She still had nightmares about it.

"It did?" Grace was staring at her with wide eyes.

"Come, sit down. You look as if you need a break." Hannah reached out and drew Grace toward the fireplace.

Grace took an armchair, opposite Hannah's, and put the towels on the floor.

"It was on the campus at my daughter's school. I found him in the bushes."

"Was it someone you knew?"

"No. He was a gardener who worked there. It was still pretty awful. I threw up before I could get myself together and notify the police. It must have been even worse for you, knowing Scott."

"It was." Her voice broke. "I don't think I can keep working here. Every time I go into that kitchen, I see him in that chair all over again."

"Have you worked here for a long time?" Hannah asked.

"Since I was fifteen. I had a part-time job on the weekends when I was in high school. When I graduated, Miss Wells offered me a full-time job. It was when Mr. Nilsson first came and they were becoming a big success. There aren't many jobs on this island and I didn't want to work in my parents' café."

"Can you think of any reason someone would want Scott Nilsson dead?" Hannah asked.

Grace chewed on her lip, eyes downcast. "Just between us, he was a bastard. He was a real perfectionist in the kitchen, and when things weren't exactly the way he wanted them, he'd yell and say the nastiest things to people."

"Did he yell at you?"

"Occasionally, he'd yell at me, but most of his temper was directed at Luke. Luke is such a nice guy and tries so hard. It made me furious the way he was treated."

"Did Luke talk back or want to leave?"

"He was planning on finding a job in Seattle and I was going to go with him. I think now he's waiting to see what Miss Wells is going to do. If she doesn't ask him to be the chef, he's out of here and I'm going with him."

"Did Miss Wells get along with Scott Nilsson?"

"Not lately. They were all lovey-dovey when he first got here. I personally thought he was seducing her into taking him on as a business partner. They even lived together for a while at her house. I think she thought he would not only be a business partner but a father substitute for Josh. Boy, did she get that wrong."

"What happened?"

"As soon as the restaurant got successful, he bought his own house, moved out of hers and started hitting on single women who came for dinner. I could tell she was furious."

"Did you ever overhear them fighting?"

"No, but I think they fought in private and he may have hit her. I saw some nasty bruises on her arms. She used to look real pretty and dress well, but after he moved out, she stopped using makeup and started wearing old, sloppy clothes. It was like she'd stopped caring about herself."

"Did her personality change?"

"She was never mean to the staff, but she always seemed either sad or crabby. In the first year he was here she smiled all the time. Now, she hardly ever does."

"What's her son like?" That question had nothing to do with the murder, but Hannah couldn't contain her curiosity.

Grace smiled. "He's a sweet, smart kid. We talk sometimes. He really loves his mom and tries to help. I think he's worried about her." She looked at her watch. "I'd better go. I have one more room to make up and then I need to help Luke in the kitchen. Thanks for being so understanding. It helps to have someone to talk to."

She picked up the towels, gave Hannah a warm smile, and left the room.

Daniel heard the door close upstairs and saw Grace walking past the second floor stairwell. Good. Hannah was alone and now they could get started with their investigation. Melanie was on the phone with FedEx arranging for a pickup. He waited until she finished the call and indicated he was heading upstairs.

"Please get me a separate receipt for my package," he said.

Melanie acknowledged the request with a nod.

When Daniel got back to their room, Hannah was seated at the desk with her iPad in front of her.

"Ready to get started?"

"Do you have a plan?" she asked.

"I think our first job is to dig deeply into Scott Nilsson's life and create a timeline. We need to know everything available online. This was a well-planned and personal murder by someone here at Alder house. Once we have his timeline, we can research everyone else here and see what overlaps. How about I do all the law enforcement databases and Facebook, and you start with Google?"

"Neither one of us is on Facebook," Hannah said.

"I have an account I use for investigations. It's remarkable how much you can find out about people you don't know."

"Okay, then. Let's get going." She turned away from him and booted up her device, her back stiff and unyielding. He was glad to have her help, but she was making it obvious he was still in very hot water.

14

THE TWO DETECTIVES WERE TREATING themselves to a late lunch at the island's only café. Elias took a large bite of a thick ham and gruyere sandwich on a crusty baguette. He always thought better on a full stomach. Rashida dug into a tuna niçoise salad.

"I wish I had a brilliant idea of what to do next," Elias said. "It's obvious that someone at Alder house is responsible for this but I'm not sure how much more we're going to get from interviews. It's not like any of them is going to confess."

"Maybe the forensics will show something," Rashida suggested.

"Like fingerprints on the chocolate?"

"I doubt it. This is a smart killer and I get the sense that this murder was well planned. Is there anyone you feel confident about eliminating?"

"I told the Suttons they could go home," Elias said. "They arrived after the chocolates mysteriously appeared in the kitchen, and Craig Sutton was negotiating a lease for a restaurant space in Seattle, contingent upon Scott Nilsson agreeing to be the chef. He's just lost a large amount of money. I can't see a motive."

"Agreed. Anyway, if you change your mind about them, you know where they live."

Elias signaled the waitress to refill his glass of iced tea. "At the moment, my leading suspects are Melanie Wells, Luke Murray, Noel Gunderson, Kylie Evans, and Ilana Flores."

"What about Daniel Ross?"

Elias disliked big city cops who always looked down on detectives from small jurisdictions. Daniel Ross hadn't said anything arrogant but Elias was imagining that he was a know-it-all, just waiting for Elias and Rashida to make a mistake.

"I hadn't considered him seriously until I found out he'd screwed Melanie and was probably the father of her kid. That puts him on the list."

"I think you're overreaching because you don't like him. If he's about to be hit up for child support, why would he do something to reduce Melanie's income? Your theory that he wanted to reunite with her and take over Scott's half of the business doesn't make sense. He's on his honeymoon. His wife is smart and beautiful. Why would he bring her here?"

Elias sighed. "You do have a point, but being a suspect will keep him from prying into my investigation, so I'm not taking him off my list."

"It's your list. How about we finish lunch and take the next ferry back to the mainland?"

"Good idea. I'm about ready to find a friendly judge and get a search warrant. Tomorrow, we'll see if the guest rooms yield anything useful."

"I need a break." Hannah shut down her iPad and gathered a few pieces of paper on which she'd been writing.

Daniel looked at his watch. "It's almost appetizer time. Do you want to compare notes?"

"Sure." What Hannah really wanted to do was lie down and put a pillow over her head. She wasn't hungry.

Daniel logged out. "What have you learned?"

"There are a great many puff pieces about him in foodie magazines. Apparently, after graduating high school in 1988, he went to the University of Illinois at Chicago on a scholarship and majored in Nutrition Science. He transferred two years later to the Culinary Institute in New York where he got his degree. He did several paid internships in Europe: Paris, Rome, and Florence. According to the articles, he trained in Michelin-rated restaurants."

"Did any of the articles specify which restaurants?"

"No, but they got specific when he returned to New York and started working at Chez Amis, a small, well-regarded upper Westside French bistro. He started there in '95, became the top chef two years later, and stayed until 2000 when the restaurant closed."

"Any idea why it closed?"

"According to one interview he gave, the owner was ready to retire. Restaurants in New York turn over pretty quickly. People always want the newest, hippest place."

"What then?"

"He took over the kitchen at Century, a boutique hotel in Chicago, and stayed there for four years until he was recruited by Mon Cher in Seattle. In 2011, he went out on his own, opening the restaurant at Alder House. There were lots of laudatory comments about how extraordinarily creative his cuisine was, drawing from the local farms, gardens, and fisheries. What did you find?"

"I looked up all the public documents I could think of and the law enforcement databases. He was born in 1970 in Chicago, at an address that suggests his family was working class. He has a juvenile record in 1986, but it's sealed so I don't know what he was arrested for. I also found a marriage certificate. In 1998, he married a woman named Evelyn Brooks."

"Were they divorced?"

"I couldn't find a divorce or legal separation agreement, so I looked for a death certificate. She died in 2000 of a drug overdose. It was deemed accidental."

Hannah raised her eyebrows. Daniel's search had certainly been productive. "The name Brooks sounds familiar. I think one of the women in the writer's group is named Brooks."

She closed her eyes and tried to envision their conversation two nights ago with the four writers. "Vanessa, the young one with the pearls."

"I hadn't remembered that. Thanks."

"She looks as if she's in her late twenties. Vanessa would have been a child when Evelyn Brooks died."

"Hang on. Let me see if I can find birth certificates."

Hannah got up, stretched, and paced the room while Daniel turned back to his computer. If they were going downstairs in a few minutes, she had better change and comb her hair. She rummaged in the closet and replaced her T-shirt with a cinnamon-colored cashmere sweater, and her sneakers with brown leather boots.

"Got it," Daniel said. "Sisters, ten years apart. Born in San Francisco. Nob Hill address."

Hannah drew a brush through her tangled hair. "That's a pretty wealthy end of town. Was there a will?"

"Let's see."

She hoped this wouldn't take too much longer. She needed to go downstairs and stretch her legs. This had been a miserable day.

"There was. She had a trust fund and guess who inherited?"

"Scott Nilsson? I wonder if her family contested the will."

"I can find that out," Daniel said.

"Not now," Hannah said. "We're both stressed out and tired. I prescribe a glass, or maybe two, of good wine for you and no murder discussions until tomorrow."

Daniel logged out. "You're right. I appreciate your help."

Hannah just shrugged.

When they walked into the lounge, Luke Murray was arranging appetizers and wine glasses. Daniel headed in his direction. The sight of food was making his stomach rumble.

"Should I get you some wine?" he asked Hannah.

"I'd rather have tea," she said, walking toward the other side of the room where the urns of coffee and hot water were kept.

Late afternoon tea wasn't one of Hannah's routines, but Daniel supposed she was limiting alcohol because of the pregnancy. He wondered if she had gotten out of the way to give him a chance to talk to Luke before any of the other guests appeared.

"Those are locally sourced cheeses," Luke said, pointing out a cheese tray decorated with dried fruit and accompanied by thin slices of French bread.

"Looks good," Daniel said, helping himself to a large sample. "How are you managing in the kitchen without Mr. Nilsson?"

"Not a problem," Luke said. "I can cook dinner for seven people with one hand tied behind me."

"Seven?" Daniel asked.

"The Suttons left this afternoon. I guess the police weren't interested in them."

"Do you know why?"

"The cops think that Nilsson died eating some truffles that mysteriously appeared in the kitchen Monday morning. The Suttons arrived Monday afternoon."

"So did we," Daniel pointed out.

"Why are you still here? I would have imagined all the guests who weren't told to stay would have left by now."

"We're still here because it's our honeymoon and we made

reservations for a week. Are you going to be out of a job with the restaurant closed?"

Luke shrugged. "The restaurant's always been closed during the winter season but it's so busy the rest of the year that, in the past, it generated more than enough money. The B&B stays open, and I always did the cooking for guests so Scott could take advantage of the free time for multiple vacations."

"Will you take over as chef when the restaurant reopens?" Daniel asked, pouring himself a glass of Malbec.

"I'm thinking of moving somewhere with more interesting opportunities. This is a pretty isolated and boring island."

"Do you have any idea of who might have wanted Scott Nilsson dead," Daniel asked, sipping his wine.

"The guy was a prick. The possibilities are endless. I doubt anyone besides Melanie will miss him."

"Was she in love with him?"

"He was her meal ticket and she was screwing him. Would you call that love?"

"I'd call that self-interest," Daniel said.

"I'd better get back to dinner," Luke said.

Daniel walked across the room and sat down beside Hannah, putting a large plate of appetizers in front of her. She was sipping at a mug of tea.

"Luke have anything interesting to say?"

"His story was pretty consistent with Grace's. Scott was a bastard. Luke's planning to leave and find a better job. It doesn't seem as if he has much to gain from Scott's death unless they have a past history we haven't uncovered yet."

"We can do a background check on him tomorrow."

Hannah cut a slice of cheese, brought it to her mouth and put it down. "I'm not hungry. I think I'll go outside for a few minutes."

"Shall I come with you?"

"Finish your wine."

Daniel watched her place her mug on the side table and

walk to the front door. He'd seen her tense, sad and depressed before, but they'd always been on the same team and he'd always been able to comfort her. This was different and he didn't know what he could say or do to make it any better.

Hannah stepped out onto the front porch and looked in the direction of the water. The sun was low in the sky and the clouds were tinged with pink over the silver of the bay. A soft breeze ruffled her hair. A creaking sound caught her attention, and she realized that someone was seated in the rocking chair on the corner of the porch. It was Vanessa Brooks.

"Hello," Hannah said, walking over and sinking into a cushioned wicker chair. "I almost didn't see you there. Lovely, isn't it?"

Vanessa smiled. "It is soothing, a balm for a stressful day."

"Did the police grill you too?" Hannah asked.

"They questioned all of us again. I can't imagine what they were expecting to learn from me. I never even met the guy who was murdered."

"This wasn't exactly how I was planning to spend my honeymoon," Hannah said. "Are you and your friends managing to get some writing done?"

"We are. I think Ilana, who is a mystery writer, is getting a kick out of observing real detectives in action."

"Samantha mentioned you were writing a memoir. You seem awfully young to be doing that. I always imagine memoir writers as having gray hair and wrinkles."

Vanessa smiled, and as Hannah watched, her face settled into a sad, faraway expression.

"Writing a memoir is like therapy, only cheaper. I'm trying to capture what happens in a family when a child dies."

"I'm so sorry," Hannah said. "You lost a child, or a sibling?"

"My older sister. She died of what was supposedly an accidental drug overdose when she was only twenty-two. I was twelve when it happened and my parents didn't tell me the truth until years later."

"You said supposedly. Do you have doubts about it being accidental?"

"My sister married at twenty-one. That was the age when she got control of her trust fund. My parents had money. When she died a year later, her will left all her money to her husband. What twenty-two year old makes a will?"

"What was her husband like?"

"I never saw him. Evelyn was studying art in New York when she met him, and apparently, they had a whirlwind romance and eloped. I do remember my parents were very upset about it. They knew nothing about his background or family. They flew to New York to meet him and weren't impressed."

"Did they think he wasn't good enough for your sister?"

"My mother described him as good-looking and shifty; the kind of guy who could be charming and lie with a perfectly straight face. My father thought he had the makings of a con man. I think he engaged a private detective to see if he had a record."

"Did he?"

"My father never said."

"Did your parents think he had something to do with your sister's death?"

"They were convinced that he was responsible for hooking her on cocaine, and that she died either because he made her so miserable she committed suicide, or because he deliberately gave her an overdose."

"Did the police find any evidence to suggest that your parents were right?"

"I don't think they tried very hard. My parents went to court to overturn the will but they lost. Her bastard husband got a considerable sum of money."

"Her death must have been devastating for all of you," Hannah said.

"You can't even imagine. My parents were so depressed and angry, they had no time for me at all. I missed her terribly; still do. Evelyn was like a second mother to me when I was little. She spent much more time playing with me than my mother did, and I was so upset when she chose to go to New York for college. I couldn't wait to be old enough to follow her."

"That's a lot to write about. Do you have any idea what happened to the husband?"

Vanessa shook her head. "I don't want to know, but I hope that he's dead in a gutter somewhere. I think I'm ready for a a glass or three of wine. Are you coming in?"

"In a few minutes. I'm going to stretch my legs before it gets too cold."

Hannah walked down the driveway, crossed the road to the beach and stood there for a few minutes, taking deep breaths. She still had that horrible knot in the pit of her stomach that had nothing to do with being pregnant, and she didn't think she could tolerate trying to make cheerful conversation over dinner. She certainly wasn't hungry. When she got back to the B&B, she would tell Daniel she was skipping dinner and retreat to their room. Hopefully, tomorrow would be a quiet day without the police.

"I hate this!" Elias Lindstrom slammed down the phone receiver.

He was busy working his way through a list of judges, trying to find one who was still in his office this late in the afternoon, and who would sign off on his stack of search warrants. He was planning to get back to the island with an evidence team first thing in the morning and search Scott's home, Luke's home, Melanie's home, and most of the B&B, including the rooms of all the writers, Gunderson and Daniel Ross. He would also love to search the guests' homes, but Gunderson was the only one who lived in his jurisdiction.

"No luck?" Rashida asked from the other side of the room.

"Not yet."

"I've got the forensics back. You're not going to like it."

"What?"

"There were plenty of fingerprints on the truffle box; Luke, Grace, and Craig Sutton. All of them admitted to eating some, so there's no smoking gun there. The fingerprints in the kitchen were all staff and Melanie. There weren't any that couldn't be explained."

"Any hair or fibers of interest?"

"Nothing on Scott or his clothes, but you wouldn't expect any. The killer did this at a distance."

"Shit. I'll keep calling. Eventually I'll find us a judge. What a fricking waste of time."

Luke had done an excellent job on dinner. The appetizer was an arugula salad with local cherry tomatoes, pine nuts, local goat cheese and a lemon dressing. This was followed by albacore tuna steaks with grilled artichokes, olives, capers and a tomato coulis. Dessert was a butterscotch crème brulée.

Daniel tried to enjoy the superb meal and pay attention to the dinner table conversation, but mostly, he picked at his food and wondered what Hannah was doing upstairs. Clearly there was more to talk about and he was steeling himself for his return to their room.

Turning down the offer of an after-dinner liqueur, Daniel climbed the stairs to the second floor. When he opened the door, the room was dark except for firelight. Hannah was curled up on one of the armchairs in front of the fireplace. She looked up when he opened the door, and even in the poor light he could tell she'd been crying.

"Sweetheart," he said. He stood in front of her, afraid to touch her.

"I've been thinking ahead," she said.

"About the paternity test?" He didn't think anything else would have elicited tears.

"I always assumed that after Annie, and before me, you had lots of sexual partners. I never asked, because once we became a couple, it didn't matter."

"I never asked you either about other men. It was hard enough competing with all your memories of Ben."

"There was no one before or after Ben. I was too busy with Zoe. I didn't care if there had been other women in your life, but I do care about Melanie. If this paternity test is positive, it changes everything."

"We've faced major problems together before. Can't we somehow work through this one?" Daniel pulled the other chair close to her and sat down, so they were face to face.

"Have you thought this through, Daniel? Assuming the test is positive, do you intend to do anything other than send Melanie money? Josh is a kid who has never had a father. Do you want a relationship with him? Do you want him to spend time with us? How do I explain him to Zoe? Having a baby brother or sister is going to be a pretty big adjustment for a six-year-old only child. How do I spring a teenage boy on her?"

"Hannah, I can't answer all those questions. I haven't thought that far ahead."

"Meaning what?"

"Meaning, if the test is positive, I know I need to take financial responsibility. As for the rest, Melanie may not want to tell him I'm his father and may not want me to have anything to do with him. In order to spend time with him, I might have to take her to court. I don't need to make that decision until I know the test results. And it isn't a decision I would make without discussing it with you."

"So, you do realize that I have feelings about unexpectedly acquiring a teenaged stepson?"

"Of course, I do. I don't know what I can do to make this better. I just know that I love you, and I don't want to lose you and our baby."

"Right now, I'm too upset to think straight. I can't begin to deal with any of this. Let's let it be, at least until tomorrow."

15

ALTHOUGH SHE HAD FALLEN ASLEEP WITH her back facing Daniel, Hannah woke finding her head, as usual, resting on his shoulder. He was still slumbering. She gently disentangled herself and tiptoed to the bathroom, where she brushed her teeth, combed her hair, and splashed her face with cold water. A night's sleep had erased the puffiness around her eyes. Careful not to wake him, she dressed and left the room.

The enticing smells of coffee and bacon wafted up the stairwell as she descended. Having skipped dinner the night before, she was famished. The breakfast buffet was already set out, and the dining room was thankfully empty. She wasn't in the mood to chitchat with other guests on an empty stomach. She helped herself to a freshly baked blueberry scone with butter and jam, a serving of crisp bacon, and a large mug of decaf coffee, then took her food into the lounge, in front of the fireplace. Through the large windows she could see that it was raining heavily. Since she suspected they would be spending their day indoors on their computers, she welcomed the bad weather. It would keep both their minds on the investigation.

The next person to come down was Noel Gunderson. Much as she disliked him, seeing what information she could extract was an interesting challenge, so she gave him a warm smile and said "good morning."

He glanced through the windows. "Not such a good morning. Lousy for fishing."

"True. It's more of a 'sit by the fire and read a good book' kind of day."

Gunderson helped himself to a huge pile of scrambled eggs and bacon and a bran muffin. "Mind if I join you?"

Hannah indicated the chair across from her. No way did she want this guy on the same sofa. "How much longer are you planning to stay?"

"I'd love to get back to Bellingham today, but the cops don't want me to leave the island."

"Do you know why?"

"They seem to consider me a suspect."

"Why would you have wanted Scott Nilsson dead?"

"I didn't. He was a great chef and he did exceptional things to the fish I caught."

"Can they make you stay here without arresting and charging you? That doesn't seem right to me. Is it legal?"

"You know, little lady, that is a good point. I should call my lawyer this morning and find out. I live in Bellingham. They know where to find me. Why the hell should I stay here until they figure out I didn't kill Scott?"

"What do you do in Bellingham, Mr. Gunderson?"

"I own the biggest sporting goods store in town and I sell lots of guns. If I wanted someone dead, I'd shoot him. I wouldn't kill him with a truffle."

Hannah laughed. "Well said. You knew Scott Nilsson for several years. Do you have any theory about who might have wanted him dead?"

"I'd look for a woman. Scott was a real player and he wasn't very nice. If he wanted a woman, he'd be Mister Charming and then dump her as soon as he got bored. I'll bet there are a great many angry broads out there who would have loved to see him dead, and truffles strike me as a woman's weapon."

"Do you think Melanie Wells could have done it?"

"I think Scott treated her like shit but she needed him too badly to kill him. Her restaurant will close without him."

Gunderson finished his breakfast and took a final gulp of his coffee. "I think I'll go upstairs and leave a message for my lawyer. Thanks for the suggestion."

"Anytime." Hannah watched as he climbed the stairs and wondered when Daniel was coming down.

Daniel woke to the sound of rain, the smell of coffee, and the realization that he was alone in the room. Hannah must have gone down to breakfast. He shaved and dressed and hurried to join her, worried that she was still upset and angry.

The first person he saw when he reached the ground floor was Melanie, seated at her desk. It occurred to Daniel that if he was Josh's father, it would be a good idea to try to diffuse her anger by being nicer. He wanted to keep his possible parental options open.

"Good morning, Melanie," he said.

"I wouldn't call it good."

"I know this is a rough time for you. Luke told me you had so many cancellations once the media publicized Scott's death, you had to close the restaurant this weekend. I am sorry."

"Not as sorry as I am. I'm not sure the restaurant will ever recover, but it would have gone down in any case. Do you know what the cops told me? That bastard Scott was about to open his own restaurant in Seattle, funded by that Sutton couple, and he was going to leave me in the lurch."

"You didn't know he was thinking of leaving?"

"No idea."

"Can Luke take over the kitchen? He made a great meal last

night. It shouldn't be too hard to hire some sous-chefs to help him."

"Luke is a very good chef but he's an unknown. People aren't going to drive up here from Seattle to eat Luke's food. If I can't attract a celebrity chef, it's over, and getting someone of that caliber, willing to live and work on a small island, is close to impossible."

"How did you manage before Scott came?"

Melanie sighed. "I ran a modest B&B on a small budget and made just enough money to make ends meet. The restaurant was a godsend. I was finally able to save something for Josh's education and for emergencies."

"Melanie, you don't know me at all. We had a one day relationship, but if the paternity test comes up positive, I will do the right thing. I'm not a deadbeat and I will help you and Josh however I can."

"Really?"

"I promise."

Hannah looked up as Daniel walked into the lounge. "Finally made it to breakfast?"

"I guess I was tired. What's good?"

"Everything. Hope it's still hot."

She watched him help himself to a big bowl of oatmeal with all the fixings and a plate of crisp bacon. He brought it over to the coffee table, filled a mug with black coffee, and sat down next to her.

"I've picked up some interesting information," he said.

"Me too, but let's discuss it all in private. I don't want anyone overhearing and the writer's group just sat down at the dining room table."

Daniel dug into his breakfast, finishing quickly, and the two of them went upstairs.

Once in the bedroom, they exchanged information.

"So," Hannah said. "We know from Grace that Melanie and Scott didn't get along and he may have abused her. That would give her a motive for murder if she wasn't dependent on him for the success of their mutual business. If she knew he was leaving, and lied to you about when she learned it, she would have had nothing to lose and a good deal to gain by killing him."

Hannah was hoping Melanie wasn't the killer. The worst case scenario was a positive paternity test, Melanie in jail, and she and Daniel having to integrate a teenager into their fledgling family.

"I can't disagree with that argument," Daniel said. "Vanessa also has a strong motive and she lied to you about knowing Scott. The only question in my mind is did she know he had a peanut allergy? If her sister married Scott when Vanessa was only twelve, it's hard to imagine how she could have learned that."

"Then there's Gunderson," Hannah said. "Much as I dislike him, I can't see that he has much to gain from Scott's death, and I don't imagine him committing murder so subtly. I see him as more of a gun, knife, fist kind of guy; a man who would kill in anger, not one who would plan so far ahead."

"Agreed. Let's talk about Luke. He could have been motivated by wanting Scott's job, knew he was allergic to peanuts, and undoubtedly has the skill to make the truffles and the access to leave them in the kitchen. We only have his word that he found them when he came to work Monday morning," Daniel said.

"True, but there was no guarantee that Melanie would promote him to chef, and in fact, she isn't going to. Both he and Grace expressed a desire to leave the island. If he was going to quit anyway, why murder his boss?" Hannah turned on her iPad. "What do you think we should do now?"

"I think we should investigate the rest of the writers' group.

Why don't you start with Ilana Flores and I'll take Samantha Allen?"

"Samantha Allen doesn't appear to exist," Daniel said. "She has a website and Facebook page, but no online photos and no birth certificate." This was a frustrating beginning to his day.

Hannah laughed. "A name like Samantha Allen is too good to be true and perfect for a romance writer. Her real name is probably something like Agnes Dogg. Why don't you check the copyrights on some of her books. I'll bet her real name is on there somewhere."

"You are a genius. Any luck with Ilana Flores?"

"Yes. She's from Washington State and got a culinary degree at the Skagit Valley College in Mount Vernon, Washington. She did an internship at a restaurant in Bellingham, and was then hired as a sous-chef at Mon Cher in 2004, at the same time that Scott was the chef. She left there a year later and went to Calexico, a nouvelle-Mexican place. You wouldn't happen to know someone at Seattle PD, would you?"

"I do. One of the detectives from the West LA station moved up to Seattle a few years ago. Why?"

"I'd love to know a little more about why she left, and any information we can glean about employees who might have had a grudge against Nilsson. Does this detective owe you a favor?"

"I'll make the call."

"I'll start researching Kylie Evans."

16

Detectives Lindstrom and James, along with an evidence team, arrived later that morning and began by presenting a search warrant to Melanie for the B&B and her home. She glared at them, furious. How much more of this would she have to tolerate?

"What do you expect to find? A bloody glove in the desk drawer?"

Elias just raised his eyebrows.

"Rashida, take an evidence tech with you to Miss Wells' house. The rest of us will start here. I'd like to do your office first, and I'll need your computer and your phone."

"How do you expect me to run my business if you take my computer," she said. "All my reservations are on it."

"I'll tell you what," Elias removed a USB stick from his pocket. "I can download all your files to this and leave the computer here, with your signed permission of course."

Melanie got up from her desk chair and motioned Elias to sit down.

"What about my phone?"

"We'll get it back to you as soon as we're done with it.

You've got a landline. Why don't you have a seat in the lounge while we're searching? We'll try not to make a mess."

"Like the neat job you did in the kitchen?"

"That was different," he said. "The kitchen was a crime scene."

"May we have your house key, Miss Wells," Rashida asked. "Or would you prefer to walk over with us and let us in?"

Melanie took the key from her purse. "You'd better finish the house before Josh comes home from school at three thirty," she said.

She didn't want her son drawn into this fiasco and she was pretty sure there was nothing incriminating in her home. Let the bastards waste their time.

"I'm starting to get hungry," Daniel said. "Would you like to go to the café for lunch? Or should I ask Luke to make us some sandwiches?"

Hannah hadn't said a word all morning. He was hoping she would talk to him at lunch.

Hannah glanced out the window. "Let's save the café for a sunny day. It's still pouring. Want to tell me what you found out about Samantha?"

"Her real name is Mildred Hunter."

"Would you read a romance novel by someone named Mildred?"

"I wouldn't read a romance novel at all, but there's so much more. Mildred is a distinguished professor of history at the University of Chicago. She was married to a politician named Bernard Hunter. He was in the Illinois State Senate and he died in 2003. The obituary didn't mention how he died, so I looked up the death certificate. Bernard took an overdose of barbiturates and the conclusion was suicide. I took the liberty of accessing the Chicago police report. You'll never guess where he died."

Hannah gave him an interested look. "I can't imagine, but if I wait patiently, I'm sure you'll tell me."

"He was in a room at the Century Hotel where Scott Nilsson was the chef. I can't believe that was a coincidence."

"So you're suggesting that Scott is somehow implicated in the death of Mildred's husband?"

"That's exactly what I'm suggesting. I'm going to see if I can get in touch with the detective who handled the case, and see if he had any ideas about the reason for the suicide, or any doubts that it was suicide."

"I'm impressed. I haven't uncovered anything as interesting about Kylie, other than the fact that she and Scott Nilsson attended the Culinary Institute at exactly the same time. I wish you had a squad of junior detectives. You could set them to tracing their other classmates and finding out if there's any history between Kylie and Scott."

"I'm afraid we're on our own here. At this point, we might learn more by engaging people in conversation. You seem to have developed that skill to a fine art. So, about lunch…"

"Let's eat," Hannah said.

Hannah and Daniel entered the empty lounge. While she poured herself a glass of ice water, Daniel opened the kitchen door and greeted Luke. The smell of something baking was tantalizing.

"Any chance for a couple of sandwiches?"

"Sure. Roast beef and cheese okay?"

"Perfect."

Luke sliced a baguette into four sandwich-sized pieces and spread them with mustard. He took thin slices of rare roast beef from the refrigerator and topped them with gruyere, slices of tomato and a sprinkling of salad greens. Sliding the two sandwiches onto plates, he handed them to Daniel.

"Many thanks. How are you holding up?"

"I was doing fine until the damn police showed up again."

"Again?" Daniel was surprised. "What did they want this time?"

"They've got a warrant to search Alder House. They're in Melanie's office at the moment and boy, is she pissed."

Daniel raised his eyebrows. He was not pleased at this news.

"I wish they'd hurry up and solve this," he said. "Thanks again for the lunch."

Leaving the kitchen, he motioned to Hannah.

"Let's go upstairs and eat there."

"Why? It's more comfortable here."

"Elias Lindstrom is back with a warrant for the B&B, which may include our room. I don't want him to find out we've been investigating his case."

Hannah followed him back to their room and watched as he locked the door.

"Can he take our computer and phones?"

"It depends on the warrant. The judge typically limits what detectives can take. You have to show probable cause that your search will reveal criminal activity. I think it would be a stretch for Lindstrom to argue that either one of us was a suspect serious enough to necessitate taking our devices, but I can't guarantee it."

"Do you think I should destroy the notes I took?" Hannah asked.

"You have a right to be looking up publicly available information about our fellow guests, but it might be best to avoid annoying him. If we discover anything truly significant, I'll feel obligated to share it."

"Got it," she said, gathering her notes. "I'd hate to annoy the local police. Don't you think it's a perfect rainy afternoon for a fire?"

Melanie Well's farmhouse was a white, shingled, single-story cottage with green trim. It was in need of a paint job. Rashida knew from the background check that Melanie had inherited the farm and the B&B from her grandparents. It appeared that little in the way of exterior maintenance had been done.

She opened the door and entered a small foyer with the evidence technician. Coats, down jackets, windbreakers and rain gear were hanging from a series of large hooks on the wall. Below the coats was a pile of rain boots.

An old-fashioned living room was to the right of the hall. A plump sofa faced a white brick fireplace, and was covered in a faded print slipcover. An old oak rocking chair with a cracked brown leather seat, and a chintz-covered armchair flanked it. A vase filled with dried pussy willows decorated the mantel, and two green china lamps with yellowed shades sat on mismatched side tables. There was dust on the wood coffee table.

To the left was a family room furnished in a matching black vinyl suite of reclining furniture and a flat-screen TV. This room looked lived in. Newspapers and magazines were strewn over the coffee table and floor. In the corner sat a desk, a computer, and a file cabinet.

"Why don't you start in here?" Rashida suggested to the evidence technician. "We're looking for any files connecting Melanie to Scott Nilsson: contracts, tax returns, etcetera. You know the drill. We should also copy all the files on the computer. I'll check the kitchen and bedroom."

It was the kitchen that interested Rashida the most. She was looking for evidence that Melanie could have created the truffles. The kitchen was also a vintage throwback. The cabinets were simple wood, painted a pale yellow. There was a farmhouse sink, an old gas stove and equally old refrigerator. The only modern appliance was a microwave.

Melanie didn't seem to be a neat freak. There were unwashed dishes in the sink and the remains of breakfast on the kitchen table. A forlorn clean bowl occupied the dish drainer.

Rashida put on a pair of latex gloves and started opening cabinets in a search for cookbooks and fine baking chocolate. All she found was a dog-eared edition of the Joy of Cooking circa 1965. The pantry contained cereals, cookies, chips and canned goods, nothing that couldn't be opened and eaten immediately. The refrigerator was equally unrewarding. The freezer was filled with frozen pizza and Weight Watcher's meals.

Melanie owned a few frying pans and sauce pans, but nothing for baking or cookie sheets. Despite an exhaustive search, Rashida found no candy thermometer. Clearly, Melanie had told the truth about not cooking. This did not totally exonerate her in Rashida's mind. She could have commissioned the truffles and left them in the Alder House kitchen. Melanie was one of the few suspects who admitted knowing about Scott's allergy.

The master bedroom contained an unmade, queen-sized bed with built-in night tables and an old oak dresser. The only interesting items in the night tables were a box of condoms, lubricant, and a vibrator. No intimate diaries. The dresser drawers were messy, which made them easy to search, and yielded nothing of interest.

Melanie's closet seemed to express two sides of her personality. On the left: comfortable jeans, sweats and slacks with oversized tops and sweaters, clearly her work clothes. On the right: several low-cut silk nightgowns, and a collection of dresses designed to cling to every curve. The few pockets in her clothes were empty and nothing was concealed in her shoes or purses.

Rashida took a quick look into the bathroom, finding birth control pills, aspirin and Tums tablets.

The second bedroom clearly belonged to Melanie's teenaged

son. She could tell by the mess and the music posters, and decided it was unlikely that anything incriminating would be found.

When she returned to the family room, she found the evidence tech boxing up a pile of files and the computer.

"We'd better give her a detailed receipt for all of this," she said.

"Find anything?"

"Not anything I was looking for. Hopefully, Elias had better luck."

Elias and Rashida placed the boxes of files from Melanie's home and office in the back of the police van and locked it. He listened as she described the house and the disappointing results of her search.

"What do you want to do next?" Rashida asked.

"Let's you and I go upstairs and do the guest rooms. We can send the techs to start on Scott Nilsson's home, and then we can do Luke Murray's. I'm particularly interested in his kitchen."

Elias was hoping something of interest would turn up. So far, he'd also found nothing.

"Unfortunately, we got a picky judge. He's allowing us to confiscate electronics from the two women who have a prior connection to Scott, and from Gunderson, but not from any of the others. We can search their rooms, but I doubt we'll find a supply of leftover truffles in any of them."

"What about Daniel Ross?" she asked.

"I couldn't convince the judge that he might have a motive."

"You couldn't convince me that he had a motive," Rashida said. "Where do you want to begin searching?"

"Let's do the romance writer," he said. "That should be quick."

Samantha Allen was at her computer, in the midst of editing a very explicit erotic fantasy, when she heard a knock on the door. Annoyed at having her concentration disrupted, she got up and opened it.

"Detective? I thought you were done here."

"I'm afraid not, Dr. Hunter. I have a warrant to search Alder House including all the guest rooms. Could you please wait in the lounge while we search yours?"

Samantha was not intimidated. "May I see your warrant, please?"

Elias handed it to her and she put on her reading glasses to peruse it.

"Fine. I'll just take my laptop downstairs and finish what I was doing while you search. If I'm not mistaken, this warrant does not give you permission to search my computer or phone. Incidentally, the first draft of my new novel is printed out and sitting on the desk. If I find out that the boys at the station are reading and posting the sex scenes, there will be an intellectual property lawsuit."

Samantha stuck her phone in the back pocket of her jeans, closed the lid on her laptop, and tucking it under her arm, made an exit.

As soon as she reached the lounge, she called each of her fellow writers.

"The Detectives are back and they have a warrant that includes your electronics," she told Kylie and Ilana. "I suggest you back up your work, delete this phone call and anything else you don't want them to see before they get to your room."

She deleted all her recent calls, poured herself some black coffee, and sat down to await developments.

17

WITHIN HALF AN HOUR, THE ENTIRE writers group was gathered in front of the fireplace in the lounge. All of them were clutching their computers.

"This wasn't what I signed on for when we chose this place," Kylie said. "Maybe we should just pack it in and go home."

Samantha, who had read the warrant, was relieved to see that no computers had been confiscated. "You wouldn't want to deprive Ilana of the opportunity to watch real live cops in action. We can read this scene in her next novel."

"The only reason the cops let me keep my computer was that I agreed to let them download all my files. If they're looking for truffle recipes, they won't find any," Ilana said.

"Did you murder any chefs in your next novel?" Vanessa asked.

"Fortunately, not. The chef in my novels is my heroine."

"Did anyone else let the detectives back up their files?" Samantha asked.

"I had to," Kylie said.

"They didn't ask me. I wonder why," Vanessa said.

"I think the warrant targeted those of us who knew Scott

previously, however superficially. The judge probably told them they didn't have grounds to confiscate my computer or yours," Samantha said.

"It's such a shame. I was really making good progress on my memoir," Vanessa said. "Do all the rest of you want to go home?"

"I think we should stand our ground," Samantha said. "We have nothing to hide and I, for one, want to finish my rewrites. I have a deadline to meet."

"The thing that pisses me off the most," Kylie said, "is that those damned detectives now have a copy of the first half of my new novel. I don't even show my husband my work until it's been edited."

"I wouldn't worry," Ilana said. "Your stuff is too high brow for those cops. My mysteries on the other hand..."

"I had a first draft printed out and on my desk," Samantha said. "I will be livid if they take it."

"I think it would do that tight-ass Lindstrom some good to read your sex scenes," Kylie said. "Well, if we aren't leaving, why don't we all get some work done?"

It wasn't long afterwards when Daniel and Hannah came down the stairs.

"Ah, another set of refugees from the search party," Samantha said, motioning them over. "Do sit down and have some coffee. Are you as peeved as we are?"

Neither one of them was smiling, nor were they holding hands. Clearly, they were also rattled by recent events.

"I can't imagine what they think they'll find in our room," Hannah said.

"I don't suppose that this so-called murder could just be an accident," Kylie said. "Maybe some grateful guest made her extra-special recipe for homemade truffles and had no idea that peanuts could kill him."

"Exactly what are the usual ingredients?" Daniel asked.

"Very high quality dark or milk chocolate, cream and flavoring. One can add vanilla, a liqueur, a fruit puree etc. The truffle balls can be rolled in any kind of nut chips or cocoa," Ilana said.

"If there were nuts on top, wouldn't Nilsson have avoided eating them? Might someone add peanut butter or peanut oil to the recipe to get the favor without the crunch?" Hannah asked.

"Certainly possible. I don't understand why the detectives are assuming a premeditated murder." Kylie turned to Daniel. "I understand you're a detective. Maybe you can explain their thinking.

"It's not my case," Daniel said. "I know as little as you do. The only thing I heard was that the chocolates mysteriously appeared in the kitchen on Monday morning and no one seems to know who sent them. That does suggest some premeditation."

"So they're looking for evidence of truffle production in our bedrooms?" Samantha asked. "Seems like a waste of time to me." They certainly weren't going to find anything in her bedroom.

"They're probably just being thorough," Hannah said.

Daniel was pacing around the room and paused at the windows. "Hey, it's finally stopped raining," he said. "Feel like some fresh air, Hannah?"

"Definitely, I've been feeling caged all day. Let's go."

Hannah took a deep breath. Rays of sunlight were peeking out from behind the clouds and causing the drops on the leaves to shimmer. A brisk breeze came off the water and she wished that she'd thought to bring a coat from her room. She pulled her sweater tightly around her shoulders.

"Chilly?" Daniel asked. He put an arm around her. She stiffened but didn't extricate herself from the warmth of his body.

"Let's get out of view of the house," she said. "I have a phone call I want to make."

"To whom?"

"Your partner, Brenda, at the LAPD. I have a favor to ask."

"Are you going to tell me?"

Hannah reached into her sweater pocket and removed a sheet of paper, which she unfolded. "I was doing some more research on Kylie. I didn't think I could access an alumni list for the Culinary Institute, so I worked backwards. I searched for famous chefs who trained there and worked in LA or Seattle. Then I looked up each of them, and found a chef in Los Angeles who graduated at the same time she and Scott did. I thought we could ask Brenda to do some digging. The chef is a woman. Perhaps she and Kylie were friends."

"You are totally wasted as a gynecologist," Daniel said, as she took out her phone. "Would you like me to make the call?"

"I'll do it." She walked toward the water, searching for the maximum number of bars before she made the connection.

While Hannah was calling Brenda, she noticed Daniel making a call as well. When she finished, he walked over to join her.

"Did you reach Brenda?" he asked.

"She's on it. She's making dinner reservations at the restaurant and we're picking up the tab. She wanted to know why the hell you and I can't go anywhere without running into a murder. Who were you phoning?"

"The detective in Chicago PD who handled the Bernard Hunter suicide. He didn't recall the case, but said he'd review the file and see if he could give me any additional facts. It was interesting that he didn't say anything about Lindstrom getting in touch with him. I wonder if the Bellingham team hasn't made that connection."

Hannah began a slow walk along the water's edge and

Daniel kept pace with her. This was all his fault. If he'd taken her to Hawaii for their honeymoon, they'd be lying in the warm tropical sun this afternoon and making passionate love at night, but he'd thought Hawaii was too banal, and she'd told him to surprise her with the honeymoon plans. Well, she certainly had been surprised.

She turned toward him. "Did you notice how quickly Ilana gave us the recipe for truffles?"

"I did. Do you think she's the one?"

"I don't know. Vanessa's the one with the compelling motive, but maybe we just don't know all of the Scott and Ilana story yet. What do you think?"

Hannah paused in her walk and looked over the water to where the mountains of the Olympic Peninsula were beginning to emerge from the low-lying clouds.

"I'd be willing to bet that the killer is one of those four women," Daniel said, "but I don't know if we can get enough evidence to identify which one."

"Let's go back inside," Hannah said. "I'm chilly and I could use some hot tea."

Grace Campbell opened the oven, pulled out the sheet of chocolate chip cookies that Luke had baked, and set it out to cool. She'd been in the kitchen with him all afternoon, helping him prepare for dinner. It was nice, just the two of them, working in companionable silence. He was teaching her the finer points of cooking, and without Scott's presence, it almost felt as if they were married and in their own home.

Luke was making chicken with a fig balsamic sauce and individual vegetable pies with filo pastry. He'd whipped up the cookies when he noticed the guests gathering in the lounge. The smell was enticing. Grace took out a serving tray and arranged the cookies on it, leaving a few for the two of them on the cookie sheet. The problem spending all this time cooking was the temptation to taste everything. She could imagine herself gaining quite a few pounds if she wasn't careful.

She carried the tray into the lounge where the four women were seated, listening to the youngest one reading. The honeymoon couple were seated together, in a corner, mugs in their hands. The reader paused when she saw Grace.

"I thought you'd enjoy some of these with your tea," Grace said, smiling as she placed the tray on the coffee table between them.

"Thank you. They smell divine," said the stocky, gray-haired woman.

As Grace looked at the group, a memory jarred loose. Who was it she had seen going up the stairs that morning? Was it the tall skinny one, the young one, the plump one, or the one with the wild curly hair? She closed her eyes for a moment as she walked into the dining room, trying to visualize the scene again. Yes, that was right. She was almost certain.

"Luke," she said, as she entered the kitchen, "I've just remembered something. Monday morning, when I came in early to set up for breakfast, I think I saw one of those women going up the front stairs. Do you think I should tell the detectives?"

"Who was it?" Luke asked.

"I'm not one hundred percent sure. I need to think about it some more and I don't want to get anyone in trouble unnecessarily. It may have nothing to do with Scott's death."

"I'd wait to tell anyone until you're certain about who and when it was. You come in early every day. What if it wasn't Monday morning?"

"I'm sure it was Monday, but you're right. I have to be positive if I'm going to tell the police I may have seen the person who left the truffles."

Elias was feeling frustrated. The search of the guest rooms had been completely unproductive. The only mildly interesting finding was that all four of the women had gloves in the pockets of their coats at a time of year when gloves weren't usually necessary.

"I wouldn't make too much of that," Rashida said. "I leave my gloves in my parka pocket all year round so I always have them when I need them."

"Maybe so, but I took them anyway. The lab hasn't finished processing the paper recycling we took. Maybe they'll find gift wrap paper with trace fibers. At least two of the gloves were wool. The others were leather."

"Worth a shot," Rashida said. "Let's go process Luke Murray's kitchen."

Luke's cottage was set in the woods on the side of the highway closest to the water. A steep hillside led down to a rocky shore, and the house was accessed by a set of steps built into the hillside. The interior was one large room with an attached bathroom. An unmade sofa bed faced the fireplace. The only other furniture was a chest of drawers, a small bookcase, and a kitchen table. The kitchen was laid out along one wall and the table served as counter space.

"It doesn't look as if he's preparing any gourmet meals here," Elias commented.

Rashida was browsing through the books. Almost all of them were cookbooks; Julia Child, Escoffier, The Silver Palate, and a large assortment of ethnic cuisines. She looked for books on baking and candy making, but found nothing.

Elias opened the refrigerator and freezer, finding primarily breakfast food. The cabinets had a few canned goods and olive oil, along with rice, lentils, beans and quinoa. He saw no chocolate, nuts or peanut oil.

They finished checking all the dresser drawers and pockets of Luke's clothing as well as the bathroom contents. No surprises.

"No evidence that the truffles were made here," he said.

"Let's see if the techs have finished with Scott's house," Rashida said. "I'm ready to head back and start going through all the evidence we've collected."

"We're going to have to dig deeper," Elias said. "We know the killer is in that B&B and I still don't have a prime suspect."

As soon as the police had finished searching the B&B, Melanie hurried home in order to be there when Josh came back from school, and to see what was missing. The first thing she noticed was that the family room seemed unusually neat. Her computer was closed and on her desk. The magazines that had been scattered over the tables and floor had been picked up and placed in a neat pile on the coffee table. A large number of files had been taken from her file cabinet.

The kitchen looked undisturbed and nothing appeared to be missing from the drawers or cabinets. Unfortunately, the police hadn't washed her dirty dishes. Melanie ran hot water into the sink, squirted in some dishwashing liquid, and left the mess to soak while she checked the bedrooms.

No sign of disturbance in Josh's room. She could tell that her drawers and closet had been searched, but once again, couldn't identify anything that the police had confiscated. Detective Lindstrom had promised her a signed receipt for everything they'd taken as evidence before they left the island.

Returning to the kitchen, she loaded the dishwasher, trying to keep her fury in check. It was bad enough that Scott was dead and that he'd been planning to betray her. The cops were adding insult to injury. And to top it off, she had Daniel Ross to deal with. She didn't trust his promises for one minute. As soon as the test came back positive, he would try to weasel out of paying her what she deserved. Men were all alike.

The front door slammed and she heard Josh's footsteps heading for the kitchen. Taking a deep breath, she pasted a smile on her face.

"Hey, Mom."

"How was school?" She asked that every day and usually got the same answer. *Fine.*

"Everyone was talking about Scott today and asking me questions. I didn't know what to say. I don't know anything. Do the police know who did it?"

"I wish. Then they'd leave. They were here all day searching Alder house and our house. They suspect everyone."

"Even us?" Josh's eyes grew wide.

Melanie walked to the refrigerator, poured him a glass of milk, and set it and a box of Oreos on the table.

"Not you, but all the adults, including me."

"That's silly. You liked Scott."

This wasn't entirely true, but Melanie didn't want to go there. "You did too."

"No, I didn't Mom. He always ignored me and he was mean to Luke and Grace. I'm sorry he's dead, but I won't miss him."

"I'll miss his cooking," Melanie said.

Josh crunched down on a cookie, scattering crumbs on the table. "When you hire a new chef, Mom, could you pick someone nice?"

Melanie walked over, stood behind him, put her arms around her son's shoulders, and kissed the top of his head. "I'll do my best."

She would bring Josh back to the B&B this evening when she returned to supervise dinner. There was a killer on the loose, and until all those guests left or the police solved the murder, she didn't want to leave her son alone.

18

DINNER THAT NIGHT WAS A GLUM AFFAIR. Despite the excellent food, no one felt much like talking. Grace served them silently. Hannah thought she seemed nervous and went out of her way to thank her. She felt sorry for Grace. Hannah knew that it took a long time for someone to recover from finding a murdered body.

Noel Gunderson appeared to be shoveling food into his mouth at top speed.

"I'll be leaving right after dinner," he announced to the table.

"The police said you could go?" Hannah asked.

"The police ordered me to get back to Bellingham tonight. They want to search my home tomorrow, the bastards."

"They're just doing their job," Kylie said. "I still think they're not going to find any evidence that Scott Nilsson's death was anything but an accident."

"Amen to that." The comment came from Melanie Wells, who had entered the dining room followed by her son. "I hope you're all enjoying your dinner."

Hannah looked at the boy closely. His features favored his mother, although it was possible that the shock of dark hair and the penetrating blue eyes came from Daniel. She wasn't certain, but she'd know soon enough. The two of them walked past her and into the kitchen.

"Hey Luke, guess what," Josh said.

"What, Sport?" Luke grinned and ruffled his hair. Apart from Grace, Josh was the only person Luke would miss when he left.

"The sky is completely clear and there's no moon."

"And you're mentioning this because…?" Grace asked.

"It's a perfect night for looking at Saturn and Jupiter with the telescope Mom got me for my birthday," Josh said. "Want to come over after dinner and see?"

Luke hesitated.

"Go on. I know you want to. I'll take care of the dishes and the breakfast setup," Grace said.

"Mom, could I ask some of the guests if they'd like to come too?"

"Why not?" Melanie said. "They all look bored. Maybe they'd find it interesting."

Much to Melanie's surprise, all of the guests, except for Gunderson who was leaving, agreed to walk over to their home after dinner for a look through Josh's telescope. The telescope had been the perfect present. Who would have imagined that she'd given birth to a budding astronomer? Josh had been obsessed with watching Nova shows on TV about cosmology and he'd excelled in math and science at school. Melanie couldn't imagine where he'd gotten those talents.

"You're so lucky to have one," Daniel said. "I always wanted a telescope when I was your age."

"Josh," Melanie said. "This is Mr. Ross."

"It's the best birthday present ever," Josh said, smiling at his mother.

Melanie watched him with pride. She would do right by her son, whatever it took.

After dinner, all the guests put on warm coats and boots appropriate for the still muddy road and followed Luke to Melanie's farmhouse. Daniel felt nervous. This was his first opportunity to interact with the boy who might be his son and he wasn't sure of how to act. He also didn't know how Hannah was feeling. Her face gave nothing away.

The night was cold and clear, and the absence of city lights revealed a sky packed with stars. Melanie met them on the front porch, ushered them inside, and escorted them through the back door of her kitchen onto a wooden deck where Josh was standing beside a large amateur telescope.

"I've got it focused on Saturn," he said. "You can see rings and some of the moons!"

One by one, the guests looked and admired. Josh refocused on Jupiter.

"Recently," Daniel said, "I had the opportunity to meet a number of astronomers. They were all looking for planets around distant stars. One of them had even discovered traces of water and oxygen on an earth-sized planet."

Unfortunately, that astronomer had been murdered, but Daniel saw no need to mention that fact.

"You mean the Kepler mission," Josh said. "I know about that. Did you know they're launching another space telescope soon that's going to focus on the stars closest to Earth?"

"I didn't know that," Daniel said. "Do you read a lot about astronomy?"

"As much as I can. I think it's the most interesting science."

"I can count four moons," Hannah said as she looked through the scope.

"I know," Josh said. "Isn't it spectacular?"

"Can you find Mars?" Samantha asked.

"Not tonight. It isn't visible right now, and it's so much smaller."

"Can I see other stars up close?" Ilana asked.

"If you point it at a star, it won't look much bigger, because it's so far away, but you will see lots more stars that aren't visible to the naked eye. Want to try?"

Over the next few minutes, everyone looked at distant stars.

"Well," Samantha said. "It's past my bedtime. Thank you, Josh, for a very interesting evening."

The four writers followed Samantha through the house and along the road to the B&B. Daniel felt reluctant to leave and Hannah didn't press him. Luke was sitting comfortably on a deck chair with a cup of tea.

"Do you need help putting the telescope away?" Daniel asked.

"You can help me carry it into my room," Josh said. "I can't leave it out because it might rain."

"This is Washington. It will rain," Daniel said.

The two of them lifted the telescope and carried it back inside. Daniel looked with interest at Josh's room. The walls were covered with posters of rock bands and Hubble Telescope photos. Daniel's teenaged room had been decorated with athletic posters.

"I see you like music. Do you play an instrument?"

"Not really. I'd love to learn guitar but there's no one on the island who could give me lessons. Maybe I can get one when I start high school."

"Is there a high school on the island?"

"Not enough kids. There's one on the mainland, about half an hour away. I'll have to take the ferry and a bus."

"Do you like living here?" Daniel asked.

"I used to. It's getting pretty boring," Josh said.

Daniel wondered what Josh would make of Los Angeles, and how he would react if the paternity test was positive.

"Daniel, we should probably be getting back." Hannah was standing in the doorway.

"You're right," Daniel said. "It was very nice meeting you, Josh, and the telescope was great."

"Thanks," Josh said.

Daniel followed Hannah out the door where Luke, with his flashlight, joined them. The three of them walked slowly back to Alder House.

Luke watched as Hannah and Daniel headed up the stairs to their room. They seemed to be a nice couple. Too bad their honeymoon had been disrupted by Scott's death. Mrs. Ross seemed tense.

Luke noticed that all the dishes were done and the dining room table was set. He didn't see Grace. He turned out the lights, locked the doors, and headed outside. That was when he noticed that Grace's old Volkswagen was still in its parking place. How odd. Where was she?

He returned to the house and called out for her, searching each of the downstairs rooms. She wasn't inside. He noticed that there were fresh bags in the trash compactor, so she must have taken the garbage out. Luke walked through the mud room, out the back door and around the side of the house where the large garbage bins were. Just behind the blue plastic recycling container, he saw Grace, lying in a heap, her head resting in a pool of blood. Luke stared at her in horror and then sprinted for the house to get help.

Hannah's cell phone rang as they entered the bedroom.

"It's Brenda," she said to Daniel as she answered the call.

"How was dinner? Glad to hear it. Did you learn anything useful?"

She paced the room as she talked. "No kidding. That is immensely helpful. Thank you. Definitely worth our treating you two to a gourmet meal."

Hannah disconnected the call and placed the cell on her bedside table. As she turned to Daniel, there was a loud knocking at their door.

"Help me. Please help." It was Luke's voice.

Daniel opened the door. Luke's face was white and tears were streaming down his face. "I think she's dead."

"Who?"

"Grace. She's lying there covered in blood."

Daniel followed Luke out the door and Hannah grabbed her emergency medical pack and followed. The three of them ran around to the side of the house. Daniel paused, holding Luke back.

"Have you checked to see if she has a pulse?" he asked.

"No."

"I'll do it," Hannah said.

Daniel illuminated the ground with his flashlight and motioned to Hannah to walk where no footprints were obvious. She knelt down next to Grace and placed two fingers on the side of her neck.

"She's alive," Hannah said.

"Should we bring her inside?" Luke asked.

"Not yet," Hannah said. "It's dangerous to move someone who may have a fractured skull, or spine injury, without proper support. Luke, go inside, call 911 and tell them we need an ambulance. Then I need you to bring me some vinyl gloves, clean towels, blankets, and a bowl of water."

Luke ran back to the house.

Grace was lying on her back, eyes closed, face pale in the beam.

Hannah opened the lid of her left eye. "Shine the light directly at her."

Daniel complied and Hannah repeated the move on the other side, exhaling a breath. "Her pupils are the same size and responding to light. That means she doesn't have a massive brain hemorrhage."

Hannah turned Grace's head very gently, exposing a long scalp laceration. "Daniel, open the pack of gauze and hand me some."

Using the gauze pads, she put pressure on the laceration and held firm, slowing the bleeding to an ooze.

"It'll take a few minutes of pressure for the vessels to clot. Then I'll see if it feels like a skull fracture and if she's wounded anywhere else."

Luke had arrived with the requested supplies and a down quilt. "There's an ambulance on its way, but they're coming from the mainland, so it will be a while. Is she going to be okay?" He tucked the quilt around her.

"She'll need a CT scan when she gets to the hospital to see whether the skull is fractured and if there's any bleeding into the brain. If there isn't, then it may just be a concussion and the world's worst headache. If there is bleeding, she'll need surgery."

"Was this an accident?" Luke asked.

"I don't think this was an accident," Daniel said. There isn't a rock or anything sharp underneath her, just dirt. I think she was attacked."

"Someone did this to keep her quiet," Luke said. "This is my fault. I should have told her to speak to the police as soon as she remembered."

"Remembered what?" Daniel asked.

"When she came in, before dawn on Monday morning, she saw someone walking up the stairs to the second floor. It was one of the women in the writing group. Grace thought she might have put the truffles in the kitchen."

"Who?"

"She didn't tell me. She wanted to be absolutely certain of her memory before causing trouble."

"Grace was alone in the house until the women got back from Melanie's," Daniel said. "One of them must have done this, but how would they have known?"

"They were all in the lounge when Grace told me about it in the kitchen. Maybe one of them walked into the dining room and overheard our conversation," Luke said.

"The bleeding's stopped," Hannah said.

She drew on a pair of gloves, dipped a towel into water, and gently cleaned Grace's head until she could get a good look at the wound.

"It's going to need stitches and I don't have any sutures here. I'll just pull it together with some tape for now."

She cleaned and disinfected the wound, shaved a few patches of hair around it, and put it together with some butterfly tape. After putting a clean towel on the ground, Hannah gently lowered Grace's head and proceeded to take her vital signs.

"Her blood pressure is 90/60. That's on the low side but not dangerous. Her heartbeat's steady."

She turned to Luke. "No sign of any other injuries. I think we can try to bring her inside now."

The three of them carried Grace through the kitchen and laid her down on the sofa in the lounge. Hannah rechecked her pupils and pulse. Grace remained unconscious.

"We need to guard her," Daniel said. "Whoever did this won't be happy to learn she's still alive."

"Don't worry," Luke said. "I'm not leaving her for a minute."

Daniel looked at his watch. It was after midnight. "Do you think it's too late to call Elias Lindstrom?"

"You probably should," Hannah said. "What about Melanie?"

"I think that can wait until morning," Daniel said. "I'll call Detective Lindstrom after the paramedics get here and we know where they're taking her."

The three of them sat, watching an unconscious Grace breathe, as they waited for the ambulance to arrive.

19

The EMTs arrived within the hour. Hannah briefed them and then stepped aside as they started an IV, rechecked Grace's vital signs, put on a neck collar and loaded her onto a gurney.

"Where are you taking her?" Hannah asked.

"To the ER at Saint Anne's, the local community hospital, for an initial evaluation. If she needs neurosurgery, we'll have to transfer her to Virginia Mason in Seattle."

"I'd like to talk to the emergency room physician," Hannah said.

"I'll connect you, Doc," the tech said, taking out his cell phone.

While Hannah waited on hold, Luke told the EMTs that he was going with them, and that Grace's parents would be waiting at the docks.

It was after 2:00 a.m. by the time the ambulance left and Daniel and Hannah returned to their room.

Hannah was exhausted. She remembered doing an emergency room rotation during residency, but it had been a long time since she'd had to deal with an acute head injury. She hoped she'd done all the right things.

"You were amazing," Daniel said. "I was so impressed that you knew exactly what to do and didn't lose your cool for a minute."

"I never lose my cool in the middle of a crisis," Hannah said. "I wait until afterward to shake in my boots."

Daniel opened his arms and she allowed herself to collapse into them, taking deep calming breaths as he held her. Finally, she pulled away.

"I forgot to tell you, Brenda had some interesting information. She met with a woman named Laura Gross, who is the chef at a new upscale restaurant in Santa Monica. Brenda told her about Scott's death and asked for background about him. The word is that Scott was an incredibly arrogant human being. He thought he was God's gift to women and probably slept with half their female classmates; the kind of guy who didn't take no for an answer."

"That's consistent with what we've been told." Daniel said.

"It gets more interesting. Laura accused Scott of raping one of her friends. The friend was at a party, remembered having a few drinks, and woke up naked in Scott's bed. Laura was convinced that Scott put a date rape drug in her friend's wine."

"Let me guess," Daniel said. "Was the friend Kylie?"

"It took a while for Brenda to extract the name, but yes. Kylie never reported the rape because she thought no one would believe her. Brenda didn't tell Laura that Kylie was a suspect."

"So, at least two of the members of the group have very strong motives for wanting Scott dead. I'm wondering what our Seattle and Chicago PD contacts have found out about the other two."

Hannah stripped off her clothes and reached for her nightgown. "I'm sure I'll be much more interested in finding out after I've had a few hours of sleep. Is Lindstrom coming here tonight?"

"No, he's going to the hospital. There's no point in trying to process a contaminated crime scene in the dark. I'm sure he'll be here first thing in the morning."

Hannah burrowed into the two down pillows and pulled the comforter over her shoulders. "Don't bother to wake me when he gets here."

Elias Lindstrom pulled his police cruiser into an empty spot in the parking lot next to Saint Anne's Hospital. Rashida James, in the passenger seat next to him, was looking bleary-eyed, despite the Starbuck's black coffee she had insisted on buying.

The two detectives walked into the emergency room entrance and Elias presented his badge to the receptionist.

"Grace Campbell, where is she?" he demanded.

The receptionist turned to her computer. "She's been transferred to the ICU, sir. It's on the fifth floor and there's an intercom at the entrance. Just identify yourself and ask to speak to the attending physician."

"Thank you," Rashida said, looking around for the elevators.

The ICU physician was a short, pudgy, balding man in a white coat with "Morgan, M.D. ICU" embroidered on the breast pocket.

"How is Grace Campbell," Elias asked. "Can she talk? She may be an important witness in a murder investigation."

"I'm sorry, Detective. She's still unconscious. She has a skull fracture and some swelling in her brain. We've started her on steroids and are keeping her sedated for now."

"How long before she wakes up?" Elias said.

"Not predictable. If the steroids don't relieve the swelling, she'll need surgery to release the pressure. It's too early to tell yet if she's going to respond."

Elias handed the doctor his card. "I'm going to assign an officer to make sure that no one has access to her except for medical staff and her family. I don't want the person who attacked her to finish the job. Please call me the minute she wakes up."

The doctor put the card in his breast pocket and disappeared into the ICU. As the door opened, Elias caught a glimpse of Luke. His face was haggard. When he spotted the two detectives, he walked toward them.

"You two better catch the bastard who did this," he said.

"Any idea of who that might be?" Elias asked.

"The only guests who were at Alder House with Grace were the four women in the writers' group. The rest of us were at Melanie's house when Grace was attacked."

"Why would one of them want to kill Grace?" Rashida asked.

"Grace saw one of them sneak up the stairs very early Monday morning. She thought the person she saw might have left the truffles in the kitchen."

"Why didn't she tell us?" Elias asked.

"She wanted to be certain of the person's identity before she said anything, and no, she didn't tell me."

"I hope she remembers when she wakes up," Elias said.

What he was thinking though, was that he hoped she didn't die before waking.

Elias handed Luke one of his cards. "I assume you'll be staying with her. Call me when she's conscious."

"Well, that was frustrating," Rashida said with a yawn as they walked down the hall. "Do you think she'll remember anything once she regains consciousness?"

Elias shrugged. Nothing in this case had been straightforward and he wasn't counting on any lucky breaks.

"I suppose you want to take the first ferry over to Oriole Island."

"I asked a couple of evidence techs to meet us at the ferry," Elias said. "I don't have much hope for the crime scene. When Daniel Ross called me, he said his wife had been working to stabilize Grace and stop the bleeding, and that he and Luke Murray had helped. Their footprints will be all over the place, but maybe we'll luck out and find whatever was used to knock her unconscious."

"Fine," Rashida said. "Before we go over there, can we please have breakfast?"

Daniel woke shortly after 6:00 a.m. Hannah was still asleep and he dressed quietly to avoid disturbing her. In truth, he'd been too agitated to sleep well. There were too many things going on and all of them were stressful.

He made his way down the stairs to the lounge, and belatedly realized that there wasn't any coffee, because Grace and Luke were both at the hospital. Entering the kitchen, he located the coffee urn, filled it with water, and found the coffee in the refrigerator. He carried the urn out to the dining room and plugged it in. While he waited for it to brew, he searched the kitchen for some breakfast. Melanie was bound to arrive soon and he didn't want to tell her the bad news on an empty stomach.

"You found Grace in a pool of blood. Grace and Luke are at the hospital and you didn't bother to call me!" Melanie shot him a furious look.

"We were a bit occupied stopping her from bleeding to death and calling for an ambulance. I didn't see the point of waking you in the middle of the night. There was nothing you could have done."

"I have a B&B full of guests expecting breakfast. I have no staff, because they're either dead or in the hospital. And you made the decision that I didn't need to know any of this before I showed up here this morning? You vanished out of my life for how many years? And then when you show back up with your new wife, you think you suddenly have the right to run my business, without my knowledge?"

"I'm sorry. I didn't mean to... Hey, I made coffee for everyone."

But she was still glaring at him.

"Fine. You're right. I wasn't thinking about the B&B. I should have let you know. I thought I was looking out for you by letting you sleep. This whole situation is a little new for me, too."

Melanie hesitated, and then finally asked. "Will Grace be all right?"

"We don't know."

"How did this happen?"

Daniel hesitated. "We don't know that either. She may have had an accident or been attacked. Detective Lindstrom will be back to evaluate the evidence."

"Why would anyone attack Grace?"

"I don't know, Melanie. Let's hope she regains consciousness and can tell us what she remembers."

Melanie pushed open the kitchen door and stormed in. Daniel followed.

"I can't take much more of this. My chef was murdered. My sous-chef is in the hospital with my waitress, who is unconscious. And then what? I'm supposed to take over the cooking?"

"I think food is the last thing on anyone's mind."

"Really? You think so? How many B&B's have you run? You think all those people are going to come down here, after not eating since last night, and not be demanding breakfast? You think I can just tell them to fast all day?"

Daniel lips narrowed. Melanie wasn't making this easy on him. "Okay. You know what your business needs. But before they all get down here, we need a plan. If Grace was attacked, one of your guests must have done it. If anyone asks, just say that Grace had an accident last night and Luke took her to the hospital. That will explain why no one's here to make breakfast. The only person who will know you're lying is the one who hit Grace on the head."

"How do I know that you didn't attack her?"

"Because Luke and Hannah and I returned here from your house together. Hannah and I went upstairs, and less than five minutes later, Luke discovered Grace and ran up to our room to ask for help. You can ask Luke if you don't believe me. I know that you couldn't have done it, because you were home during the time it must have happened."

Melanie opened the refrigerator, took out milk, a dozen eggs, a loaf of sliced bread and some butter. "I don't suppose you know how to make French Toast," she said.

"Actually, I do. By the way, I enjoyed talking to Josh last night. He seems like a smart and very nice kid."

Melanie didn't reply. She just began cracking eggs into a large bowl.

Samantha Allen pulled back the drapes and looked out the window. The sun was up, the sky was clear and it looked like it would be a beautiful day. She could smell the scent of coffee brewing downstairs and her stomach rumbled. Only two more days to go. They all had plane reservations to fly out of Bellingham on Sunday morning. She doubted the police would solve Nilsson's murder before then, and she knew there were no grounds to delay her departure or that of any of her friends.

She took a quick shower, pulled on some clothes, and headed down to breakfast. As she walked out the door, she saw Kylie approaching the stairs from the other wing, and heard the murmur of voices from the dining room.

"Did you sleep well?" Samantha asked.

"Not really. I am so ready to get out of here."

"I haven't gotten much work done either, but I don't think it's wise to leave earlier than planned. It'll look suspicious. And there's no point in calling unnecessary attention to ourselves. Don't want to give the detectives any reason to confiscate more of our things."

When they reached the dining room, Ilana and Vanessa were in the midst of breakfast, and Daniel Ross was nursing a mug of coffee. There was a bowl of fresh fruit, and Melanie was refilling a heated tray of French Toast on the sideboard.

"Is that the only option for breakfast?" Samantha asked. "I was hoping for something with fewer carbs."

"Sorry," Melanie said. "Our waitress had an accident last night, and the sous-chef is with her at the hospital. Unfortunately, on this island, there's no option for ordering take out. So, I did the cooking."

"I can make Samantha an omelet," Ilana offered, turning toward Melanie. "In fact, I'm happy to help out with dinner tonight. I'm sure the past few days have been very difficult for you."

"That is so kind of you," Melanie said.

"We'll all be out of your hair on Sunday," Vanessa said. "In the meantime, we'll try to be thoughtful guests. We can all pitch in, in the kitchen."

Samantha turned to Daniel. "Where's your wife this morning?"

"Still sleeping, I think. We're leaving on Sunday as well."

"I imagine she hadn't planned on quite so eventful a honeymoon."

"I hadn't either," he said.

Daniel stayed in the dining room, drinking coffee, and observing the four women in the writing group. He watched their faces as Melanie mentioned Grace's accident, and was unable to detect a flicker of surprise or tension. Whoever was responsible was extraordinarily calm and a very good actress.

He finished his coffee, listening to their conversation, and then decided to take a breakfast tray up to Hannah. After what she went through last night, he wasn't sure she was ready to face the four suspects at breakfast.

She was still in bed when he opened the door but her eyes were open.

"Is that coffee?"

Daniel put the tray on the small table next to the window and opened the drapes.

"Coffee and breakfast."

She smiled at him. It was the first time in days she'd done that. He felt a wave of relief.

"Give me a minute." She got out of bed and headed for the bathroom.

As Daniel waited for her, his cell rang. It was a Chicago area code. "Detective Ross, this is Rob O'Rourke at Chicago PD."

"Thanks for getting back to me."

"I pulled the file. If you give me your LAPD email, I can send it to you."

"That would be great," Daniel said. "Is there anything you can tell me now?"

"Looking at the file did jog my memory. The Century Hotel is known for its discretion. It's the sort of place well-heeled couples check into for illicit affairs. High-end hookers, of both persuasions, frequent the bar. Bernard Hunter was a regular, although he always checked in using a pseudonym."

"Was he having an affair?"

"He used the place to pick up male prostitutes. He was gay and very closeted."

"I didn't come across any of that information when I did an internet search. It's the sort of story the media feeds on."

"We kept it under wraps. He was a State Senator. I'd appreciate your confidentiality."

"Of course. Was there any doubt in your mind that it was suicide and not murder?"

"None. He did himself in with barbiturates and whiskey, and left a note in his handwriting for his wife."

"Motive?"

"His note apologized and said he couldn't stand living a double life any longer, and couldn't tolerate the hurt and embarrassment of being exposed. We think he was being blackmailed. In the two months before his death, there were several large cash withdrawals from his bank account."

"Did you ever find out who the blackmailer was?"

"We didn't. Do you think this death has a connection to your case?"

"I can't prove it yet, but yes. I don't believe in coincidences. Thank you. If you ever need help in Los Angeles, I'm your man."

As Daniel put away his cell, Hannah emerged, hair combed and face scrubbed. Sitting down, she swallowed some coffee and poured syrup on her French Toast.

"I suppose we have to wait until Lindstrom gets here. I was hoping for some fresh air and maybe a hike," she said.

"You? Hike?"

"I know it's out of character but I'm feeling trapped in this place. Everything is unresolved, and I just wish we could forget about it all and go home." Her voice began to crack, as if she were on the verge of tears.

Daniel came and stood behind her, trying to knead the tension out of her back and shoulders. "I know, sweetheart. I wish we'd never come, that I'd taken you somewhere else for our honeymoon."

"You and me, both. But it looks like we're stuck here, trying to solve a murder, and waiting for the results of your paternity test."

20

While Hannah dressed, Daniel took her breakfast tray down to the kitchen, rinsed her dishes, and put them in the dishwasher. Melanie was busy cleaning up. The dining room was empty and Daniel wondered where the writing group was meeting. He would have liked to be a fly on the wall, to listen in to their conversation.

His phone rang as he seated himself in the lounge to wait for Hannah. It was his Seattle colleague with follow-up on Ilana Flores. Daniel listened with interest. Four women and now four motives for revenge. It was time for him to tactfully pass on his information to Elias Lindstrom.

Elias and Rashida sat in their car waiting to board the ferry. Elias ended his phone call.

"Any news?" Rashida asked.

"I sent a team to search Gunderson's house. He got home last night. I left word with forensics to call me when they finish going through the recycling pile."

"I'm not optimistic," Rashida said. "We've narrowed things

down to our four female suspects but if Grace Campbell dies, or doesn't remember, I don't know where to go from here."

"Let's take it one step at a time. Maybe we'll find some useful trace at the second crime scene."

Hannah spotted Daniel on his cell, in the lounge, as she descended the stairs. She'd dressed in jeans, a long sleeved T-shirt and a windbreaker, and had slathered sunscreen on her fair skin. He hung up as she reached him.

"Ready for a walk?" he asked. "We can drive to the other side of the island. There's a trail that begins in the hills and has nice views."

"Just get me out of here before Lindstrom shows up. I need to do something normal today that has nothing to do with murder." She was hoping some physical activity would make her feel less agitated.

Daniel took her arm and guided her to the car. "Does that mean you don't want to know what I found out from my Seattle source?"

"Of course, I want to know. You can tell me while we're driving."

Daniel started the car and turned right at the highway. It was a perfect day to be outdoors. Sunlight sparkled on the water and a cool breeze drifted through the partly-opened car windows, blowing strands of her hair.

"Okay, spill it."

"The restaurant manager remembered Scott and Ilana quite well. Apparently, she burned a sauce because she wasn't paying attention and Scott went ballistic. He humiliated her in front of the entire kitchen staff and fired her on the spot. If someone in her family hadn't owned a Mexican restaurant, her career as a chef would have been over. As it is, her current job is quite a comedown from working at one of the hottest spots in Seattle."

"So, we have four suspects, all of whom have good reasons for wanting revenge on Scott. The guy was a possible rapist, a possible blackmailer who caused the death of Mildred Hunter's husband, the ex-husband of Vanessa's sister and possibly responsible for her death from a drug overdose, and the man who humiliated Ilana and ruined her career. Busy guy," Hannah said.

Daniel didn't say anything for a while, but she could tell there was something on his mind by the way he pursed his lips and drew his eyebrows together. The road had left the coastline and meandered through dense woodland, finally beginning to climb a steep hillside. A few minutes later, Daniel pulled into a turnoff with a view of the water and the Olympic peninsula.

"We're at the trailhead," he announced.

"Where does the trail go?" Hannah asked.

"It's a two mile loop with a five-hundred foot elevation gain. Are you sure you want to do it?"

Hannah wasn't at all sure. Walking uphill wasn't one of her favorite activities, but she couldn't turn down a challenge, not in her current mood.

"Let's go." She opened her door and slid out of the passenger seat.

Daniel locked the car and led the way. It wasn't long before she was short of breath, trying to keep up with his long, loping stride. After a few minutes, he looked back and waited for her to catch up.

"Why don't you set the pace?" he said. "I know you don't do this very often."

"Standing in the operating room doesn't provide much aerobic exercise," she admitted.

A few more switchbacks brought them to another viewpoint, looking over the island.

Hannah seated herself on a convenient boulder. "Would you like to tell me what's on your mind?" she said.

Daniel exhaled. "What's on my mind is that we are spending

our honeymoon with a killer. I don't want you to be alone with any of those women. The killer didn't hesitate to attack Grace and I don't want you to be next."

Hannah shot him a look. "I would think you pose the greater threat. I'm sure, whoever she is, she didn't plan on encountering an experienced homicide detective. She probably thought Scott's death would be interpreted as an accidental allergic reaction. You're the one who should be careful. I don't need protection or coddling. I can take care of myself."

Hannah got up and walked swiftly back to the trail. She didn't know if she was angry because he was hovering, or because she hadn't been able to forgive him for Melanie. She heard his phone ring, and his voice answering but she didn't slow down. No doubt, he'd have no trouble catching up.

Fifteen minutes later, she paused at the one mile marker at the crest of the trail. It was all downhill from here. So far, all the hike had accomplished was to make her legs ache and to demonstrate her bad physical condition. It hadn't helped to dissipate her stress or her anger. She heard Daniel's footsteps and watched as he reached her.

"That was Detective Lindstrom on the phone. He wants to interview us."

"No surprise."

"I told him we'd be back in about an hour."

"Just how I wanted to spend my afternoon."

"One more thing, Hannah. There's an email on my phone from the lab. The paternity results are back."

"Aren't you going to open it?" Hannah asked.

"I suppose I have to." Daniel's finger touched the screen and he waited for the PDF to load.

"Well?"

"Melanie was telling the truth. I am Josh's father."

Hannah's heart started beating faster and she blew out a deep breath. There was a tight knot in the pit of her stomach.

She'd expected the positive result, but that was different than having her fears confirmed.

"What now?" she asked.

"I have to talk to Melanie. We have to tell Josh."

"Do you?"

"I want to. He's a nice kid and he deserves more than just a monthly check from me. I want to get to know him."

"What if he doesn't want a relationship with you?"

"I won't be able to forgive myself if I don't even try."

"Suppose Melanie doesn't want him to know? They've managed just fine without you all these years."

"Biological fathers do have legal rights."

"What about our family, Daniel? You have a daughter and another child on the way. What about us?"

He reached out to touch her, but she stepped out of his reach. "I won't love you any less because I have another child. I never expected anything like this, but I'm trying to deal with it as best I can. Can't you bring yourself to help me?"

"I don't know," Hannah said. "I need some time to sort out my feelings about this. I never expected to learn on my honeymoon that the man I married isn't who I thought he was. I'm not ready to welcome Josh with open arms. I can't. Not yet."

Hannah felt tears beginning to come and fought them back. She needed a clear head and the murder wasn't helping. What she really wanted was to go home to Zoe, her practice, and her life before all of this happened.

"I think we should head back to Alder House," she said. "The detectives are expecting us."

Elias and the evidence team combed the side and back yards of Alder House looking for footprints and for the murder weapon. The previous day's rain and mud assured a plethora of footprints. They would have to sort out which ones belonged to the victim, to Luke, and to Hannah and Daniel Ross, before they could determine whether the killer had left any.

As he watched the techs making casts, Elias had a thought and returned to the inn through the back door and the mudroom, where there was a large supply of sturdy rubber boots along with rain ponchos. Examining each of them with gloved hands he found what he was looking for.

"See if these match any of the footprints," he said. "The bottoms are caked with mud."

"Where'd you find them?" Rashida asked.

"Mudroom. I suspect the killer borrowed them to avoid wearing boots that could be traced back to a specific owner. If I'm right, all we can say for sure is that the killer's feet were equal to, or smaller than, the boot size."

One of the techs examined the soles and placed the boots in a large evidence bag. "You're probably right," he said. "We still need to find out what shoes everyone else was wearing that night and match them to the footprints we've found. There are five distinct sets."

"I think I found the murder weapon," the other tech said. "It was close to the edge of the woods that bordered the backyard."

"What is it?" Elias asked.

"A rock with a sharp edge and traces of blood. The killer must have hit her and then tossed this as far away as possible."

Elias took Rashida's arm and steered her back to the house. "Time for you and I to collect everyone's shoes."

As they walked into the foyer, Elias heard the sound of a car driving up to the front door. He looked out and saw Luke slamming the driver's door closed.

"Perfect timing," he said as Luke walked in. "We have a few questions for you. How is Grace doing?"

Luke stared at them without answering for a long moment.

"She died this morning," he said.

"I'm so sorry," Elias said. "I know you were friends."

Shit, he thought, our best lead gone. We'll never solve this case.

"We were more than just friends," Luke said.

"You told us yesterday that Grace thought she knew who had placed the truffles in the kitchen. How would the killer have known Grace could identify her?"

"The only thing I can think of is that the killer must have overheard us. Voices do carry from the kitchen into the dining room. One of the women must have walked in there from the lounge, while Grace was talking."

"That makes sense. Thank you. I only need one more thing, the shoes you were wearing last night when you found Grace. There are lots of footprints back there and we need to eliminate yours."

Luke looked down at his feet. "I'm wearing them. I don't have an extra pair to change into here."

"Why don't you wait in the kitchen? I'll take them to the evidence techs for a cast, and then you can have them back," Elias said.

Luke shrugged and walked inside, just as a car drove up with the Ross couple inside.

"I need both of you to give me the shoes you were wearing last night," Elias said, as they exited the car.

"For elimination purposes?" Daniel said.

Elias nodded. "We have a lot of prints around the crime scene."

"Mine are in our room," Hannah said. "I can go upstairs and get them."

"So are mine. I'll come with you," Daniel said.

"Meet me in the lounge," Elias said, as he watched the two of them go up the stairs. They both seemed tense, hardly the loving, honeymoon couple. Despite the fact that Daniel might prove to be the father of Melanie's kid, Elias had confirmed that they hadn't been here early Monday morning and neither of them had a prior connection to Scott Nilsson.

At the moment, Elias had four viable suspects but no hard evidence. This case should have been a slam dunk and it was proving to be anything but.

"I'm hot and sweaty, and I need a shower," Hannah announced as they entered their room. "Can you take my boots down to Lindstrom?"

Her rain boots, worn the previous night, had been left in the bathroom to clean later. Daniel took them from her, careful not to touch the soles. He'd been wearing his new black Nikes last night. He was hoping Lindstrom wouldn't confiscate them.

"Sure. Lindstrom probably wants to talk to us separately anyway."

He heard the sound of the shower starting, and glimpsed Hannah divesting herself of her hiking clothes through the partly open bathroom door.

"I'll come and get you when he's ready for you," he said, as he left the room.

There was no reply.

He noticed Melanie at the front desk when he reached the ground floor, and acknowledged her with a brief smile, before joining Elias in the lounge. He'd have to talk to her later today and he wasn't looking forward to it.

He held out the shoes to Elias, who placed each of them in separate evidence bags.

"Any chance of getting those back before we leave tomorrow?" Daniel asked.

"I'll have my guys do casts and return them. You and your wife aren't suspects in this case."

"Glad to hear it."

"Tell me what happened last night, in detail, from the beginning." Elias took out his notebook and Daniel complied. His story and timeline were consistent with Luke's, as was his recounting of Luke's theory on why Grace was attacked.

"How is she doing this morning?" Daniel asked.

"She's dead. We're looking at a double murder here."

"You know," Daniel mused, "it's almost as if we have two separate killers."

"How so?" Elias asked.

"The first crime was meticulously planned and organized by someone who knew of Scott's allergy. The second crime strikes me as a murder of opportunity by a killer who was panicked at the thought of being revealed. Could this be a two person project?"

"Sounds like the same person to me. The killer had time to plan the first murder, but not the second. There are only two people who had a prior connection to Scott, Ilana Flores and Kylie Evans," Elias said. "Both of them could have known about his allergy, and Flores is a chef. She could have made the truffles, but we haven't been able to find a motive."

Daniel took a deep breath. "Detective Lindstrom, I know this is your case and your jurisdiction, and I have no wish to step on your toes, but my curiosity got the better of me. I did some research, and called in a few favors in LA, Seattle and Chicago. I found possible motives for all four women."

Daniel summarized his findings, hoping that Elias wouldn't be too offended to listen.

"Food for thought," Elias finally said. "I'll need my guys to confirm everything you've found and to dig much deeper into the death of Bernard Hunter. That connection is dicey. You have given me some new questions to ask my suspects."

"I hope you're not angry," Daniel said.

"At this point, I'll take all the help I can get. One more question. Luke thinks that whoever attacked Grace might have overheard the two of them talking in the kitchen. When you and Mrs. Ross were in the lounge yesterday, did you notice anyone going into the dining room?"

"I'm afraid not. I wasn't facing in that direction, but Hannah was. Perhaps she noticed something. Should I ask her to come down?"

"Please," Elias said.

21

Hannah was tying the shoelaces on her sneakers when Daniel came to get her. She'd washed her hair, twisted it into a bun, and changed to slacks and her favorite dark green sweater. Her face was bare of makeup, and despite having worn a hat on their hike, Hannah was afraid she would break out in freckles at any moment.

"Lindstrom would like to talk to you now," Daniel said.

"What did he ask you?"

"Just a recounting of last night's timeline, so he can be sure everyone is telling the same story."

"Did you tell him everything we'd discovered?"

"I did."

"Was he angry?"

"If he was, he didn't show it. There were clearly things he didn't know and he's having his team double check our findings. I didn't tell him that you were involved in the investigation. I didn't want him pissed off at you too."

Hannah shrugged. She didn't need credit for her sleuthing skills. She just wanted all of this to be over. "I'd better go downstairs."

"One more thing you need to know. Grace died this morning."

"Oh, no." Hannah's eyes filled with tears. She wasn't used to losing patients. Her specialty was birth, not death. "Did I miss something?"

Daniel reached over and brushed a tear from the corner of her eye. "You did everything you could have done under the most difficult circumstances, and you weren't in charge in the ICU. Don't even think about blaming yourself for any of this."

"I'm not. I'm just so sad that a lovely young woman is dead."

"Me too." Daniel drew her into a quick hug. "Come on, I'll walk you down."

Daniel paused at the foot of the stairs and watched Hannah as she walked around the corner to the lounge. Once she was out of sight, he turned to Melanie.

"Can we talk?" Daniel asked.

She looked up from her computer. "Sure."

"In private."

Melanie raised her eyebrows, got up, led Daniel into her small office and closed the door.

"I got the results this morning. I am Josh's biological father," Daniel said.

"I told you, you were."

"I'm still trying to get used to this, because it wasn't something I expected, but I will try to do the right thing. I'm hoping you and I can come to a fair financial agreement without involving lawyers." Daniel watched her face. Her expression was suspicious.

"What do you propose?"

"When I get home, I'll put together all the documentation for my finances and you put together information about your expenses. We can agree to find a mediator to work with us to negotiate child support payments. I'd also like to start a college fund for Josh."

Her face relaxed slightly. "That sounds reasonable. What do you want out of this arrangement?"

"Access. I want you to tell Josh the truth and I'd like to have a relationship with him, if he's willing." Daniel tried to imagine how he would have felt as a teenager to discover he had a father who had never been part of his life. Would he have been curious, or resentful, or both?

"Joint custody is off the table," Melanie said.

"I'm not asking for that. I'd like to be able to visit and get to know him, and to have him come to Los Angeles once or twice a year to spend time with me and with my family."

"Has your wife agreed to this?"

"Hannah is still processing the fact that her new husband has a son he never knew existed, but she's a very warm and loving person, so I'm pretty sure she'll be okay with it."

Daniel hoped that was true. What he feared was that he may have permanently lost her trust and perhaps even her love. He couldn't stand to think about that. He'd never, in their years together, seen her so anxious and aloof.

"I hope you're right," Melanie said, "because I won't allow Josh to go anywhere he isn't welcome."

"He will be," Daniel said.

"I'll tell him when he comes home from school. You can come over and talk to him after dinner."

"Please, sit down, Dr. Kline," Lindstrom said, waving her to an armchair.

Hannah thought Lindstrom looked exhausted. She'd seen that look all too often on Daniel.

"My husband just told me about Grace. I'm so sorry."

"I understand you did a heroic job administering first aid and getting her to the hospital. Now that we are dealing with a double murder, it's even more crucial that I have your cooperation."

"Of course."

He asked her to review the timeline for the previous night, along with her best recollection of who was where and at what time. Hannah did so.

"How long was it from the time you and your husband went upstairs to when Luke knocked at your door?"

"I don't think it was more than five minutes," Hannah said.

"When you examined Grace Campbell, did you think it could possibly have been an accident?"

"Not a chance. She had a large gash in her scalp that was bleeding heavily but she was lying on dirt. There was nothing underneath her that could have produced a wound like that."

"Do you have an estimate for how long she may have been lying there, or to ask the question another way, could Luke have been responsible?"

Hannah visualized Grace's body, lying in a pool of blood, and the expression on Luke's face when he came to their door.

"I'm not sure how long she was lying there, but judging by the amount of blood, she must have been attacked before the three of us returned to the B&B. Luke's distress seemed genuine to me, unless he is a superbly trained actor."

"One more question for you, Doctor," Lindstrom said. "You and your husband were in the lounge along with the writer's group while we were searching the house. Did you notice any of the women go into the dining room during that time?"

Hannah looked toward the sofas and the fireplace, remembered Grace bringing the platter of chocolate chip cookies, which were passed around and shared by the six of them. One of the women had taken the empty plate and walked to the dining room with it. Who was it? She closed her eyes and waited for the image to emerge. Then, she had it.

"Now that I think about it, I did see someone," she said.

Melanie followed the dirt road to her house, mentally rehearsing what she wanted to say to Josh. Daniel Ross had proved surprisingly accommodating about her demand for child support, although it remained to be seen if he'd stay that way once they began to negotiate in real dollars. Truthfully, she needed the money badly. If sending her son to Los Angeles for an occasional holiday was the price for the cash, Melanie would willingly pay it. She hoped her son would be tractable.

When she entered the house, the light on in the kitchen and the backpack on the hall floor informed her that Josh was already home from school. He was at the table with a glass of milk and a box of Oreos. She tousled his hair and sat down opposite him.

"Cookie?" he asked.

She accepted the offering.

"I have something important to tell you."

Josh looked up.

"Remember when you first asked me about your father? I told you he was a nice man I'd met who was in the military. We had a very short relationship and then he was discharged, and I had no idea where he was living. He never knew I was pregnant with you."

"I remember. Have you found him?" He was paying close attention now.

"I have, and he's taken a paternity test which proved definitively that he is your father."

"How did you find him?"

"He showed up by sheer coincidence as a guest at Alder House. You met him yesterday. His name is Daniel Ross."

"The detective who knows about astronomy?"

"That's the one."

Josh exhaled, blowing out a long sustained breath. "What did he say when you told him about me?"

"He was very sorry he didn't know about you until now and he'd like to spend time with you, if you're willing. He suggested you might like to visit LA during your school holidays. He's going to help support you and put you through college."

Melanie watched as Josh absorbed the information and then his face broke into a radiant smile.

"Wow, Mom. That is so great. When can I talk to him?"

"I'll invite him to come over after dinner tonight."

This might work out even better than she had hoped. If Daniel became attached to Josh, perhaps he might be persuaded to leave his new wife and they could become a real family. From where she was observing the newlyweds, the honeymoon looked as if it was over.

Hannah returned to their room, trying to put together a coherent theory of the two murders. The pieces all fit, motive, method and opportunity, but the police didn't seem to have any hard evidence that could tie the woman she'd seen in the dining room to the crimes. She had a thought about how to do that and perhaps Daniel might have an additional suggestion.

When she opened the door, Daniel was at his computer reading the LA Times.

"I'm glad you're back," he said. "I need to talk to you. While you were with Lindstrom, I spoke to Melanie."

"And?"

"We agreed to submit our mutual financials to a mediator to negotiate a child support agreement and I told her I'd start a college fund for Josh."

"On your detective's salary?"

"Hannah, you've met my parents. You know they're wealthy. My sister and I were both given trust funds which came into our control at the age of thirty-five. There's more than enough money for college for Josh, for Zoe, and for our new baby."

"Zoe won't need your money. I'll make sure she has enough for any education she wants." Hannah wasn't sure why she was feeling so prickly but she felt a great need to lash out at him. "Is Melanie going to tell him about you?"

"She said she'd talk to him when he got home from school today. And if Josh is willing to meet with me, I could go over there tonight. Would you like to come with me?"

Part of her wanted to, mostly to keep an eye on Melanie and make sure she wasn't making a play for Daniel, but her better instincts prevailed.

"I think this first meeting, as father and son, needs to be between the two of you. If he wants to spend time with you, I'll have plenty of chances to get to know him."

"That makes sense," he said.

She could almost feel his relief. He hadn't really wanted her to tag along. "On another subject, I think I know who the murderer is, and I have an idea about how to prove it."

As soon as Hannah left the lounge, Elias called for Rashida.

"Let's take a walk. We need to interview those four writers and they apparently went for a drive around the island. While we wait for them to return, I learned a few things I want to tell you about."

Elias proceeded to outline what he'd learned from Daniel Ross.

"That guy is one hell of a detective. I'm embarrassed neither of us managed to unearth that information," Rashida said. "Are you pissed?"

"Yeah. It's such a stereotype when the big city detective runs circles around the hick cop."

"You're not a hick cop. You just don't have as wide a circle of contacts as Daniel Ross. It didn't hurt that he could send his partner out investigating."

The two of them reached the rocky beach and Rashida bent down, picked up a few pieces of driftwood and began throwing them over the water. Elias found a log and sat.

"So what's your plan now?" she asked.

"I'm going to call the station and get a few guys working on confirming Ross's findings. I can't take his word for any of it. If what he said is true, Kylie Evans, Ilana Flores and Vanessa Brooks have rock solid motives for wanting Scott dead. The connection between Scott and Samantha Allen is much more tenuous. Just because her husband died in a hotel where Scott was the chef, doesn't mean there was a connection between them."

"There probably is a connection. We just haven't found it yet."

Elias sighed. "This is the most frustrating case. Our best suspect is the woman Hannah Kline saw in the dining room, but it's a long way from assuming she overheard Grace and felt threatened, to proving that she hit Grace over the head with a rock."

"Do you think the trace evidence will help?" Rashida had thrown her last piece of driftwood and walked over to sit beside her partner.

"It hasn't so far. As soon as those four women return, I'm planning to confiscate the shoes they wore last night. It's clear Grace's killer was wearing those rubber boots. I'm hoping the trace inside them matches something on someone's shoes. If we can identify Grace's killer, we can work backwards to Scott's."

"Are you going to confront them with what we know?" Rashida asked.

"Not yet. I'm going to wait for the trace evidence from the crime scene. I'll only have one chance to force the killer into a confession and I want to be sure I have enough ammunition."

"How about we get some lunch, and maybe they'll be back by the time we finish. The island isn't that big."

Dinner Friday night, prepared by Luke with some help from Ilana, was a glum meal. People helped themselves to the large Caesar salad, the butternut squash ravioli with brown butter sauce, and the blueberry crumble with a minimum of conversation apart from "pass the butter, please."

Daniel kept a careful eye on the four women in the writer's group, looking for signs of tension, but not a one of them stood out. Everyone at the table was tense, irritable, and more than ready to go home.

After dinner, Hannah returned to their room and Daniel, having received the hoped-for invitation, walked down the dirt road to Melanie's farmhouse. His knock was answered by Josh, who greeted him with a nervous, formal handshake.

"I'm not sure what to call you," Josh said.

"How about Daniel? Maybe later we can progress to Dad, once I've earned the title."

"That sounds good. Would you like to come in, Daniel?"

"Very much."

Josh led him into the living room and motioned for him to sit on the sofa.

"Would you like tea or coffee? Mom's in the kitchen. She thought we'd like to talk privately."

"I just finished dinner," Daniel said. "But I would like us to talk. I'm sure all this came as a huge surprise to you. It did to me as well. It'll take us both some time to get used to one another."

"Mom said you might want me to visit you in LA during school break. I've never been there and I'm dying to go. Could we visit Disneyland, and could I see your police station?"

"I think both of those could be arranged, if it's okay with

your Mom. We could even visit the planetarium at the Griffith Park Observatory. It has a huge telescope. I think you'd like that."

Josh grinned. "Do you have another family in Los Angeles?"

"I do. My wife Hannah is a doctor, and she has a six-year-old daughter named Zoe, who will be excited to meet you. I also have family near San Francisco. My folks will be thrilled to discover they have another grandson. But I'd love to learn more about you, Josh. Your friends, your interests, your life on the island. Please, tell me what you'd like me to know."

Daniel sat back on the sofa as Josh began to talk.

22

IT WAS RAINING ON SATURDAY morning. Elias was glad he'd decided to spend the night in a motel close to the mainland ferry dock instead of returning to Bellingham. No point in doing that long drive if they were going to have to return to the island the next day. Rashida had been in agreement, and the two of them had shared burgers and fries in the motel coffee shop before retiring to their respective rooms.

Elias was working on scrambled eggs, bacon, and coffee when his partner joined him.

"When do you want to head over to the ferry?" she asked.

"I'm not in a hurry. I'm waiting to hear from the lab. I put a rush on those rubber boots and the trace from the shoes. They'll call me when they have something."

He passed her the menu and she ordered coffee and blueberry pancakes.

"We need to wrap this up," she said.

"No kidding. We may think we know who and why, but it's not going to hold up in court without hard evidence."

"Unless we can get her to confess," Rashida suggested.

"Good luck with that."

Hannah rolled over in bed and opened her eyes. Daniel was still asleep beside her. She'd deliberately gone to bed early and feigned sleep when he returned, so that she could avoid talking about Melanie and Josh. One part of her brain thought she was being childish and unreasonable. The other part just felt resentful and far from ready to incorporate a teenaged boy into her life.

She tiptoed out of bed, brushed her teeth, and turned on the shower. Closing her eyes, she allowed the hot water to warm her body and felt the weight of her wet hair. She lathered her scalp with the lavender scented shampoo and washed the rest of her with shower gel.

As she ran her hands over her abdomen, she tried to detect even the subtlest change, but ten weeks of pregnancy hadn't affected her silhouette. Her body was soft, with generous curves, but had never been slim. Her breasts were large, tender from being pregnant, her hips generous and her clothes a size fourteen. She'd long ago given up her teenaged habit of constant dieting to match her thin friends. It was always followed by compensatory weight gain. And by the time she'd met and married Ben, she'd decided to be happy with how she looked. She'd try not to gain more than the recommended twenty-five pounds during the next seven months.

She toweled off, wrapped herself in a terrycloth robe and reentered the bedroom.

"You're up early." Daniel was smiling at her from his side of the bed.

"I went to sleep early."

"I know. You were out cold when I got back."

She knew she was supposed to ask how things went with Josh, but somehow, she couldn't bring herself to open her mouth, so she just searched in the dresser drawer for a set of underwear.

"Why don't you shower and dress? I could use some coffee."

Elias was nursing his second cup of coffee when his cell finally rang with the anticipated call from the lab. Rashida watched his face as he listened.

"Did you get what you wanted?" she asked.

"So far, so good. The trace on the inside of the boots matched the trace on the outside of one of the sets of shoes, and didn't match any of the others."

"Was it the right set of shoes?'

Elias grinned. "It was. I'm still waiting for the rest of our team to track down the information Daniel Ross gave me. I need a coherent story to tie her to both murders."

"Are you going to tell him?"

"Yeah. I think he's earned the courtesy." Elias pulled up his contact list and dialed.

Daniel was pulling on his jeans when his phone rang. He listened to Elias, nodding.

"That's good to hear. Hannah and I were talking last night. Everyone is scheduled to leave here tomorrow morning, and it would be nice to wrap this up before that happens. She had an idea about this case and I think she might be right. If you agree, here's our suggestion on how to test it."

Hannah was watching him closely from across the room as he elaborated on her theory and her suggestion for bringing the case to a close. He gave her a smile and a thumbs up, as he listened to Elias's reply and the two of them worked out the details.

"We're on for dinnertime," he told her.

"Great. I can't wait to get home."

"Let's get some breakfast, love."

Her face gave nothing away as she preceded him out the door and down the stairs. He was going to have to figure out the best time to bring up his conversation with Josh. It was pretty clear she had no desire to talk about it right now.

Later that night, when Daniel entered the dining room for dinner, everyone else was already seated. Melanie and Luke came out of the kitchen, bearing a large platter with a sliced rib roast, and set it out along with an assortment of grilled vegetables and salads.

"Why don't you and Luke sit down and join all of us for dinner?" Daniel suggested. "You've both done such an outstanding job under very difficult circumstances."

Melanie nodded in acknowledgment and seated herself at the head of the table. Luke sat in a designated chair to Melanie's right.

"This is our last supper together," Melanie said. "I'm so sorry your time with us wasn't relaxing. No one could have predicted two deaths in one week and the constant police presence. Thank you all for your forbearance. Please, help yourselves to dinner."

The four members of the writer's group, seated nearest the sideboard, got up first, followed by Daniel and Hannah, who were sitting opposite them. Melanie and Luke, at the other end of the table, waited until all the guests had served themselves.

"I assume we're all leaving in the morning?" Daniel said. "It would be good to have some answers before we scatter."

Everyone turned toward him.

"What kind of answers?" Kylie said, cutting her roast beef.

"I think all of us would like to know who murdered Scott Nilsson and Grace Campbell," Daniel said.

"I thought Grace's death was an accident," Kylie said. "I heard she fell and hit her head."

"It wasn't an accident," Hannah said. "If it had been, the police wouldn't have been here all day collecting evidence."

"I would think," Samantha said, "that solving those deaths would be up to the police. I doubt we can figure it out over dinner."

"It's clear to me," Daniel said, "that Scott's killer had to have known about his allergy, and had to have a compelling motive for desiring his death. Many of the people at this table could have known about the allergy. For example, Scott's partner, Melanie Wells. Their partnership agreement leaves her as sole owner of the B&B and the restaurant."

"That's absurd," Melanie said. "The restaurant was a huge success because of Scott. It's going to be impossible to replace him. His death was the last thing I wanted."

"Scott was going to leave here and open a restaurant in Seattle, in partnership with Mr. Sutton. They sealed the deal the night Scott died," Daniel said. "If you'd known about it, you might have been angry enough to murder him."

"But I didn't know," Melanie said. "I won't be accused in my own B&B."

Daniel knew he was angering Melanie, but he had to proceed anyway. "On the other hand, we do know you couldn't have murdered Grace," he continued. "You were at home with several witnesses when she died."

"Then, there's Luke," Hannah said. "He knew about the allergy and had been chafing under Scott's thumb. We all know that Scott Nilsson was nasty to anyone who worked under him. His death gave Luke the opportunity to become the chef instead of the underling."

"I didn't need to murder Scott to get away from him. I was planning to quit and move. Grace was going to come with me," Luke said.

"We know you couldn't have attacked Grace," Hannah said, "because you were with us until you found her."

"What about the two of you?" Samantha asked. "How do we know you aren't responsible?"

"We couldn't have been. For one thing, we'd never met Scott and knew nothing about him. For another, the truffles were placed in the kitchen very early Monday morning, and we didn't arrive until late afternoon. You ladies in the writing group arrived here on Sunday," Hannah said.

"Are you accusing one of us?" Vanessa's blue eyes were wide with indignation. "I never met Scott Nilsson. Why would I possibly want him dead?"

Vanessa's hands, on her lap, curled into tense fists.

Hannah's face was warm and sympathetic. "You know, it's very difficult to hide things from law enforcement. They have access to so many legal documents. Did you think they wouldn't learn that Scott was your brother-in-law?"

Daniel watched all their faces as Hannah dropped that bombshell. Luke and Melanie looked stunned. The other three women betrayed nothing by their expressions. He was sure this information had come as no surprise.

"I'm not lying," Vanessa said. "I never met him. I was just a teenager when he eloped with my older sister, and they lived three thousand miles away. She died not long after they were married."

"Of a drug overdose," Hannah said. "It's understandable that you and your family might have blamed Scott for that."

"We did. Evelyn never used drugs, not even when she was at Berkeley." Vanessa's eyes were beginning to water.

"Before she died, Evelyn made a will leaving her trust fund to her husband. Your parents tried to contest it and lost. It's all in the legal record," Daniel said.

"The bastard married her because she was rich, hooked her on cocaine and oxycontin, and got rid of her. You're right. I had good reason to hate him, but I didn't know he was allergic to peanuts, and I can't cook. I'm glad he's dead, but I'm not responsible."

"You aren't the only one with a motive," Daniel said, turning toward Ilana. She sat across from him, stone-faced, holding her knife and fork in a tight grip.

"You worked under him in Seattle," Hannah said. "I heard he was an absolute bastard and hated by the entire kitchen staff."

"That is correct," Ilana said. "That's why I left."

"You didn't leave voluntarily," Daniel said. "He fired you, and humiliated you in front of all your co-workers."

"Scott always liked to make an example, but I got a better job. It was the best thing that ever happened to me."

"Was it? Moving from a five-star rated restaurant to a little neighborhood café? That hardly seems like a step up."

"Any job that took me away from Scott was a step up."

"You must have been very uncomfortable at the thought of seeing him again," Hannah said.

"Why? He wouldn't have recognized me. I was just an anonymous Latina to him."

"Unfortunately, I think," Daniel said, "that you may be the leading suspect as far as the police are concerned. You worked with Scott. You must have known about his allergy. You had good reason to hate him and you can cook. You've certainly demonstrated that in the past few days."

"They can suspect me all they want. They have no proof," Ilana said.

She turned her attention to her roast beef, cut off a large chunk, and began chewing with a vengeance.

Daniel turned his attention to his meal.

Hannah finished a bite of salad and turned toward Kylie.

"You must have really despised him," Hannah said. "I can't imagine what it must have been like for you to come face-to-face with your rapist after all these years. No one ever believes the woman in that situation. They assume she was drunk and she led him on. Killing him would have given you justice."

Kylie put down her utensils and stared at Hannah, her lips tight and her eyes hard.

"I seem to have underestimated the police. But I got my justice by becoming far more successful than Scott ever was. My husband and I own and manage a whole chain of restaurants. I had no need to kill him."

"Perhaps not," Daniel said. "But you are a trained chef and could certainly have made those truffles. It's also quite likely you knew of his allergy. As a suspect, you're as good as Miss Flores."

"To quote my friend Ilana, you can suspect all you want to. The police have no proof."

Samantha Allen took a large gulp of her red wine and glared at Daniel. "Are you finished accusing us, Detective?"

"Not quite, Dr. Hunter."

"I see you've uncovered my real name. Nothing nefarious there, I'm afraid. Elderly history professors just aren't the right image for bestselling romance writers."

"I know about your husband, Dr. Hunter."

"What about my husband?"

"We learned about his suicide," Hannah said. "That must have been awful for you."

"It was, and it has nothing to do with Scott Nilsson."

"Was it just a coincidence that your husband killed himself at the Century Hotel, where Scott was working?" Daniel asked.

"What else could it have been?" Samantha's rage was showing and her voice had begun to crack.

"The Chicago police think he killed himself because he was being blackmailed, and they know why he was vulnerable. From everything I've learned about Scott Nilsson, I wouldn't put blackmail beyond him."

"You're right. I knew about my husband, and he told me Scott was blackmailing him. My mistake was not realizing that he was distraught to the point of suicide. My husband was a good, kind man. As far as I'm concerned, Scott Nilsson murdered him."

"Did you murder Scott Nilsson?"

"I didn't know about his allergy, and the only cooking I do involves take-out and a microwave."

"I have a theory about this murder," Hannah said. "You are a group of four writers who have worked together for a long time and know one another well. Each of you had a valid reason to despise Scott Nilsson, yet you chose to have your retreat at a B&B owned by the man who raped one of you, fired and humiliated another, and was probably responsible for the deaths of a sister and a husband. I can think of only one motive for coming here—revenge."

"You are formidable women," Daniel said. "And jointly, you have the knowledge and skills to plan and execute this very clever murder. I think Ilana was the one who told you about the allergy, and that either she or Kylie made the chocolates. One of you went downstairs very early Monday morning and left them in the kitchen. The only problem was that you were seen."

Daniel nodded in the direction of Luke. "Please, tell us what Grace said to you on the day she died."

Luke's eyes swept across the four women. His mouth was hard. "Grace saw one of you going upstairs as she arrived on Monday. She told me about it in the kitchen, when all of you were waiting for the detectives to search the house. She hadn't said anything earlier because she'd just remembered, and wanted to be absolutely sure of that person's identity before going to the police."

"Are you going to tell us who she saw?" Samantha asked.

"She didn't say," Luke answered.

"She was attacked to keep her from talking," Daniel said. "And one of the four of you had to have done it, because no one else was in the house."

"That doesn't help you," Kylie said. "You have suspicions, but no hard evidence to back them up."

"That's where you're wrong. The only way one of you could have learned about Grace, was if you overheard her conversation with Luke. And only one of you was in the dining room, close to the kitchen door, while Grace was in there," Hannah said.

Hannah turned to Samantha. "I saw you."

"That doesn't prove anything," Samantha said.

"There is hard evidence," Daniel said. "The killer put on a pair of Melanie's rubber boots, so that her footprints wouldn't give her away. That was a smart precaution but not smart enough. The police took trace evidence from all of our shoes, and the trace from yours matched the inside of the boot."

Samantha took a deep breath and let it out slowly. "You win. I'm sorry about Grace. That was a spontaneous decision that I regret, but I don't regret killing Scott. He didn't deserve to live."

"Are you confessing to his murder?" Daniel asked. "What about your co-conspirators?"

"They knew nothing. I learned about the allergy from Ilana and planned everything myself. I was the one who made our reservation for the retreat, and I didn't tell them that Scott was the chef until the last minute. I was afraid they would all refuse to go."

"Are you telling us that you made the truffles? I thought you couldn't cook anything that didn't involve a microwave?" Hannah asked.

"I have a PhD, for God's sake. Don't you think I'm smart enough to look up and follow a recipe?"

Daniel looked around the table. There was distress on the faces of all the women. He wondered if they were upset at discovering Samantha was a killer, or if they were feeling guilty that Samantha was taking the blame.

"It's not true," Kylie said. "I'm not letting you confess to all of this. Your PhD notwithstanding, it's not that easy to make professional-looking truffles, especially when you're adding peanut oil. It messes up the texture. I had to make several batches before I got the balance of the ingredients correct."

"All you did was make truffles. I was the one who left them in the kitchen," Samantha said.

"I don't think so," Hannah said. If you or Ilana had been seen going upstairs Monday morning, Grace would have recognized you immediately. Your heights and body types are distinct. Yet Grace was unsure. The only two women she could have confused for one another were Kylie and Vanessa, who are quite similar in height and weight."

"I won't allow anyone to take blame for me either," Vanessa said. "It was my job to leave the chocolates in the kitchen. We weren't trying to kill him, you know. We just wanted him to suffer. His death was an unexpected bonus."

"You want us to believe you didn't know someone could die from anaphylactic shock?" Daniel said.

"We knew that but we expected him to try the truffles during the day, when there were plenty of people around to give him his EpiPen, and call an ambulance. We had no idea he would wait until he was alone with a bottle of cognac to eat the chocolates," Samantha said. "In any case, I plan to confess to being the sole person responsible for this death. I asked Kylie to make chocolate truffles for me. And I asked Vanessa to drop off my present in the kitchen. Technically, they didn't do anything illegal. It was all me. I masterminded it all. They had no idea that I killed Grace to cover my tracks."

"You do know, you'll be tried for two counts of first-degree murder?" Daniel asked. "That's a life sentence."

Samantha shrugged. "I'm seventy-nine years old and I have stage four metastatic breast cancer," she said. "A life sentence won't be very long. And I'll die knowing I rid the world of a despicable human being. Are you going to arrest me now?"

"Not my jurisdiction," Daniel said. "But Detective Lindstrom is waiting outside."

He took out his phone and made the call.

It was finally over. The police had arrested Dr. Mildred Hunter and driven away. Everyone else had returned to their rooms to pack. No one had been able to finish the lovely dinner Luke had prepared.

Hannah's stomach still had that horrible feeling she associated with anticipating medical board exams, and her uterus had begun to cramp as well. She was glad she'd packed earlier that afternoon. They had an early flight to catch and an even earlier ferry. She couldn't wait to leave Oriole Island and hoped never again to set eyes on Melanie Wells.

Daniel followed her up the stairs and they entered the bedroom.

"You were brilliant," he said. "The questions you asked were worthy of a trained interrogator."

"Thanks. I am trained. It's just that my training is in asking my patients the right questions, at the right time, to help me make the right diagnosis. This process is more collaborative but the end result is often the correct answer. You're the one who reached out to your contacts to get all the key information. Are you going to let Samantha take the blame for all of it?"

"That will be up to Lindstrom and the prosecutor. It's clear she wants to protect the other three younger women, and she feels she has little to lose. I think they all thought Scott's death would be written off as an accident, and they would never be suspected."

"They didn't count on running into the best detective in the LAPD."

"And his intrepid secret partner." Daniel smiled at her and reached over to pull her close. "We haven't talked at all about my son."

"What about him?" She pulled away from his encircling arm

and faced him. "How did he take the news that you were his long lost father?"

"He was happy and excited. He's a very nice kid, Hannah, and he's spent his life on a small, isolated island. He can't wait to visit Los Angeles. I need to know that you'll be able to welcome him."

The very phrase, my son, felt like a punch in her gut. "You should know me well enough to realize I'd never be mean to any child."

"Not being mean isn't the same as being warm and caring, as you are to all your friends and your patients. I can't change the mistake I made fifteen years ago. How long are you going to be upset and angry about it?"

"I don't know, Daniel. I need some time to adjust. I assume he's not coming home with us now."

"Of course not. I was thinking, maybe winter break."

"In that case, right now, I want to wash my face, put on my nightgown and get ready for bed."

Hannah headed to the bathroom, taking her time to change, remove her makeup, brush her teeth, and empty a full bladder. As she turned to flush, she noticed the blood.

"Daniel, I'm bleeding."

His face blanched. "Are you having a miscarriage? Do we need to take you to the emergency room?"

"It's not that much blood. It may not mean anything, but I do need an ultrasound. I'll call my partner and ask her to meet us tomorrow. We can drive to my office directly from the airport."

"Are you sure?" He put his arms around her again, and this time, she didn't pull away.

Of course, she wasn't sure. The only thing she was sure of was that she didn't want to go to the emergency room of some rural hospital. She'd handled enough first trimester bleeding in her own practice to know it could be a false alarm, or it could be the first sign of a pregnancy that had failed. She blinked back her tears. The thought of losing this baby, their child, seemed much worse knowing that Daniel already had a son.

"I'm pretty sure we'll be okay waiting until tomorrow." She left his encircling arms and retrieved her phone. "I'm going to call Ruth now. Once I've had the scan, I'll know what I need to do."

23

HANNAH SLEPT FITFULLY THROUGH THE night, waking up several times to check for bleeding. Her uterine cramps remained mild and the bleeding minimal, although she knew this could change at any minute.

They had set their alarm for 5:00 a.m. in order to dress, finish packing and make the 6:00 a.m. ferry. As they left Alder House, Hannah looked back, hoping never to see it again. Daniel drove the speed limit to Bellingham airport, making only one stop at a supermarket for her to purchase thick sanitary pads, just in case things changed for the worse.

They were on time for their 9:30 a.m. flight from Bellingham to Seattle, where they endured a three hour layover before boarding the 1:00 p.m. flight to Los Angeles. As soon as they landed, she called Ruth, who promised to be waiting when they arrived.

It always felt a little odd, coming to her office on the weekend, when the building was locked, and the driveway to the parking lot closed with a gate. Daniel paused while Hannah fished her gate card from her wallet, and collected her office and building keys.

Ruth greeted them both with a hug. Hannah and Ruth had been residents together and had opened their two-woman practice as soon as they'd graduated.

"So, how was the honeymoon?"

"We ate a lot and solved two murders," Hannah said. "About what you'd expect from the two of us on vacation."

"Very funny," Ruth said.

"I wish it was a joke," Daniel said. "It's all true. I owe Hannah big time. She gets to plan all our vacations from now on."

"I can't let you two go anywhere," Ruth complained. "Tell me what's happening with the pregnancy."

"Spot bleeding, mild cramping since last night. Can you scan me?"

"Of course. Come on." Ruth led the way into the ultrasound room and turned on the machine as Hannah undressed, lay down and put her feet in the stirrups. Daniel hovered at the head of the exam table. Ruth turned off the room lights and gently introduced the ultrasound probe.

"I'm so sorry," she said, "It looks like a miscarriage."

The diagnosis had been immediately obvious to both of them, if not to Daniel. The embryo wasn't moving and had no heartbeat. Hannah turned her head away from the ultrasound screen and cried silently.

"Let me give you two a few minutes alone," Ruth said. "Then we'll figure out what to do next." She left, quietly closing the door.

Hannah felt Daniel reach out and try to hold her. She curled into a fetal position, not wanting to look at him.

"Sweetheart, it's not the end of the world. We can try again."

It was the worst thing he could have said and she had to force herself not to lash out at him. He'd just acquired a son. Not a big loss for him.

She rolled over and looked at him. To his credit, he looked devastated. "Easy for you to say. You aren't the one who has to undergo the IVF procedure."

He brushed a tear off her cheek. "What happens now?"

"D&C, in the office, either now or tomorrow, whichever Ruth would prefer."

"Not in the hospital?"

"Not necessary. She'll give me a local block and a little sedation. I'll need you to drive me home."

"Of course."

"Let's do it tomorrow morning at 7:00 a.m.," Ruth said, as she returned to the exam room. "I'll call my nurse to come in early to assist me, and you can be in and out of here before my first patient arrives. You don't have anyone scheduled before Tuesday. I can insert the laminaria now."

"What's that?" Daniel asked.

"It's a piece of sterile seaweed. It absorbs water and dilates the cervix painlessly. Why don't you wait outside while I do it? Hannah will be ready to go home in a little while."

Daniel seemed only too eager to leave, Hannah thought. Funny how a guy who didn't flinch at a crime scene got cold feet at the thought of watching a gynecologic procedure.

"Thanks for kicking him out," she said.

"Is there something you're not telling me?"

"It wasn't an ideal honeymoon and it's too long a story for now. Let's just get this over with first. Thanks for always being here when I need you."

Ruth gave Hannah another hug. "And vice versa."

As Daniel drove back home to Brentwood, Hannah fixed her makeup using the car mirror. She didn't want to look as if she'd been crying when she saw Zoe.

Daniel pulled his car into the garage and the two of them

entered the house through the kitchen. Emilia, their long-time housekeeper, was stirring something that smelled like chicken soup over the stove. Her face lit up when she saw them.

"Welcome home!"

The sound of running footsteps came down the hall and Zoe, her curly brown hair flying, sped toward them.

"Mommy, you're back. I missed you." She reached up her arms and jumped into Hannah's embrace, wrapping her legs around Hannah's waist and depositing little girl kisses on her cheeks.

"I missed you too, sweetheart. I'm so glad to be home."

Zoe turned her big brown eyes toward Daniel. "Hi, Daddy. I missed you, too."

"Glad to hear it, Princess."

"You should have taken me on your honeymoon."

Hannah grinned. Just holding Zoe in her arms had soothed her and probably lowered her systolic blood pressure by twenty points. "There weren't any other kids there. You would have been bored. I promise to take you next time we go away. Did you and Emilia have a good time?"

Hannah took a surreptitious look around. The last time she and Daniel had gone away on a romantic vacation, they'd returned to a new kitten. She was hoping Emilia hadn't added anything to the animal menagerie.

"We went to the park and the playground, and I had lots of play dates with Molly at Aunt Andrea's house."

"Sounds good. Did you learn anything new in school?"

"I'm doing a science project. It's on how babies get born."

Hannah rolled her eyes at Daniel. She hoped Zoe hadn't copied anything graphic from her medical books.

"I'm sure it will be great," Hannah said. "What's for dinner?"

"Chicken stew and chocolate cake," Emilia said. "Zoe baked it and frosted it, herself."

"Sounds wonderful. Emilia, can you stay over one more

night, and take Zoe to carpool tomorrow morning? My partner scheduled a very early surgery for us and Daniel has to leave early too. You can take the rest of Monday off. I don't have patients and I'll be home in the afternoon to be with Zoe. I can't thank you enough for staying with her."

"No problem. We had a good time. You unpack now and rest. Dinner will be ready in half an hour."

Hannah and Daniel unpacked in silence, and before he could break it, she fled into the bathroom. She'd comforted so many of her patients when they'd had miscarriages, but only now did she realize how badly they had been hurting.

The embryo may have only been an inch long, but already she'd been thinking of names, mentally decorating the nursery, and mulling over preschools. She knew she could try again but Daniel's unexpected son had changed the equation. She didn't know now if she really wanted another child, if she could trust Daniel, or if she even wanted to stay in her new marriage. The only thing she was sure of was that she was too upset to make a rational decision about anything.

"Hannah, are you all right?"

"I'm fine. I'll be right out." She splashed cold water on her face, swallowed two Motrins, and ran a comb through her hair.

"I was afraid you started bleeding more."

"I'm just having cramps from the laminaria. It'll be over tomorrow."

He reached out once again to take her in his arms. His embrace felt comforting…for now.

Early the next morning, Daniel drove Hannah to her office. He was at a loss as to how to reach her and comfort her. She seemed to be hiding behind an emotional wall and she wouldn't let him in. It didn't help that he was hurting too. He wanted a child of his own and he wanted that child with Hannah, not with Melanie, who'd been a one-night mistake when he'd been young and very unhappy.

"How long will the procedure take?" he finally asked.

"Half an hour, and I'll need a little time after that for the sedative to wear off. We should be back home by eight-thirty, so you won't be late for work."

"Are you sure you don't want me to stay with you today?"

"Positive. I'll be fine."

Daniel didn't argue. He sensed there was no point.

While Daniel waited in her private office, Hannah undressed, settled herself on the exam table, and Ruth started an IV. Ruth's nurse gave her a sympathetic glance and squeezed her hand.

"Just giving you a little sedation," Ruth said. "Try closing your eyes and tuning out. It'll be over soon."

Hannah felt the speculum being placed, a quick, cold spray of numbing medicine, and Ruth injecting the block for her cervix. While Ruth waited five minutes for the local anesthetic to take effect, she changed into another pair of sterile gloves and arranged her instruments.

"Go ahead," Hannah said. Her hands gripped the sides of the table as the sound of the suction machine began. It felt like really intense menstrual cramps, but was over in two minutes.

"I'm going to check with the ultrasound to make sure I got it all," Ruth said.

Hannah opened her eyes and glanced at the screen. "Looks good to me."

"Why don't you rest for a few minutes and I'll go tell Daniel you're okay. Do you want him to come in and keep you company until you're ready to go?"

Did she? She honestly didn't know, and it upset her that she wasn't sure if she wanted him there. On the other hand, she had to remember that he'd also lost something.

"Sure. As soon as you've finished cleaning up in here, ask him to come in. Daniel's used to the sight of blood, but not in this context."

Daniel parked his car in the garage and helped Hannah out of the passenger seat.

"Let me at least get you settled in before I leave for the station. You haven't even had coffee today."

"That's true, and I could use some to counteract the sedative."

She curled up on the sofa in the den. He covered her with an afghan and brought in her Kindle. "Coffee coming right up."

She heard the water running, and the sound of the beans grinding, followed in short order by the enticing smell of brewing coffee. In a few minutes, Daniel entered, holding a large mug.

She took a sip and felt the instant energy surge she always got from caffeine.

"Perfect, thank you." She had to keep reminding herself that his willingness to take care of her, even when she was tired and cranky, was one of his nicest qualities and one of the reasons she'd married him.

"I was just thinking how glad I am that we didn't tell anyone I was pregnant, especially Zoe and my mother."

"And mine. I thought you were being overly cautious when you said we shouldn't announce it until the second trimester, but you were right."

"It's easier if you don't have to explain a loss to people, and experience it again every time you tell someone."

He didn't say anything, just caressed her hair as she drank her coffee.

"Speaking of explaining, I have no idea how to tell Zoe about your son, or how to explain him to our friends." Every time she thought about it, she was torn between pain and anger.

"Why don't you leave that to me? It's my responsibility and it doesn't need to be done right away. We're both mourning this loss now. It isn't the right time."

"Are we both mourning? You've just acquired a brand new son. Do you even want another child?"

"I wanted our child. Didn't you?"

"Right now, I don't know what I want. It's going to take me some time, and a good deal of discussion between us, to figure it out. Why don't you head off to work? I'm feeling okay. All I need right now is a little more sleep."

Daniel just looked at her, his eyes sad. Finally, he leaned down, kissed her cheek, and left the room. She heard the sound of his car starting.

She finished her coffee and closed her eyes. They'd been married one week and she was miserable. The tears started to flow as she let it all out; the anger, the loss, the sense of betrayal, the doubts. There was too much to think about, but it could all wait. She would calm down, get back to work, let their life settle into its normal rhythms, and then she would decide whether or not to stay married.

ACKNOWLEDGMENTS

First and foremost, this novel is an homage to Agatha Christie, whose prolific and clever books first introduced me to the mystery genre. Agatha Christie invented the "English Country House" style of murder mystery, in which a limited cast of characters are in an isolated setting and a murder takes place. The reader knows that it was an inside job, and the detective must figure out which of the survivors is also a killer.

Those of you who have read my previous novels will notice that this one is quite different. It's told from multiple points of view and all of it is in the third person, unlike its predecessors, which are narrated only in Hannah and Daniel's voices. I've always wanted to try this structure, and it was great fun to write.

As always, I appreciate the wonderful help of Linda Schreyer, my editor, who always knows how to make my stories stronger and notices the mistakes I can't see.

I thank my brother, Lawrence Kreisman, who introduced me to his favorite San Juan Island, which inspired the setting for this story.

My husband, Uri, as usual, figured out the computer glitches. Attorney Jerry Bernstein made sure I didn't make any embarrassing legal errors.

Finally, kudos to designer Kristin Bryant for creating such a beautiful cover.

ABOUT THE AUTHOR

PAULA BERNSTEIN is a New York native, who migrated to LA to attend graduate school in Chemistry. She acquired a PhD, an exceptionally nice husband, and the ability to synthesize creative meals from leftovers. Not long afterwards, she escaped her laboratory and attended medical school.

Like her series heroine, Hannah Kline, Paula spent her professional life practicing Obstetrics and Gynecology. When she developed an irresistible desire for an uninterrupted nights' sleep, she retired from her full time practice, and reinvented herself as a writer of medical mysteries.

Learn more about her at her website: https://www.hannahklinemysteries.com/

ALSO BY PAULA BERNSTEIN

The Hannah Kline Mysteries

Murder in the Family

Murder by Lethal Injection

Murder in a Private School

Murder in the Goldilocks Zone

Murder In Vitro

Murder on Her Honeymoon

Short Stories

Potpourri

On Call for Murder

Non-Fiction

Carrying a Little Extra

Woman to Woman